Puffin Books

Horned Helmet

This is the story of Beorn, an Icelandic boy who runs away
from a cruel master, is befriended by Starkad the fearful
baresark Jomsviking, and joins his ship.

As the Vikings make their swift deadly raids along the
Scottish coast Beorn learns to fight, and kill, to sing their
songs, and to accept their rigid code. 'Jomsvikings are not
concerned with manners, only with truth and hard-dealing.
Never talk to a Jomsviking just for the sake of politeness. We
have sworn an oath only to say what is so; no more and no
less.'

There is no softness in this book. It is a magnificent saga
of the Norsemen, showing both their courage and brutality
with a ring of truth.

'This is a very fine historical novel. It moves at a tremendous
pace, and, without being at all consciously "poetic", has the
authentic ring of heroic poetry' – Rosemary Manning in the
Teacher

'The language is poetic and strong and seems to shout with
a love of the fierce life. The drawings by Charles Keeping are
dark as nightmares; superb. Mr Treece obviously knows what
he is talking about' – the *Yorkshire Post*

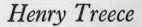

Henry Treece

HORNED HELMET

Illustrated by Charles Keeping

Puffin Books

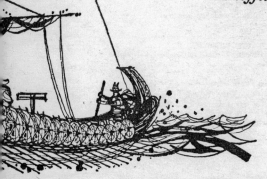

Puffin Books, Penguin Books Ltd, Harmondsworth Middlesex, England
Penguin Books, 40 West 23rd Street, New York, New York 10010, U.S.A.
Penguin Books Australia Ltd, Ringwood, Victoria, Australia
Penguin Books Canada Ltd, 2801 John Street, Markham, Ontario, Canada L3R 1B4
Penguin Books (N.Z.) Ltd, 182–190 Wairau Road, Auckland 10, New Zealand

First published by Brockhampton Press, now
Hodder & Stoughton Ltd, 1963
Published in Puffin Books 1965
Reprinted 1968, 1970, 1972, 1974, 1975,
1976, 1978, 1980, 1984

Made and printed in Great Britain by
Richard Clay (The Chaucer Press) Ltd, Bungay, Suffolk
Set in Monotype Plantin

Contents

Author's Note

Iceland was known to sea-faring Irish monks quite
early on; but it was not until 867 that a Norwegian
Viking, called Naddodd, discovered the island, when
his longship was driven off-course on the way to the
Faroes.

After that, Vikings (or 'wanderers') from all parts of
Scandinavia, the Hebrides, and Ireland went to settle
there, to farm and to fish, and often to escape punishment for crimes they had committed elsewhere!

Between the years 930 and 1260, these independent
'Icelanders' created a form of rough law and self-
government that was quite amazing – especially when
we remember that they did not become Christians until
the year 1000.

We can learn all about this from the Icelandic stories called sagas. I have tried to write *Horned Helmet* in the style of the sagas, as far as possible, so that you can get the feel of these old tales.

The Northmen, whether they came from Scandinavia or Iceland, were often very intelligent people, with a rough dry sense of humour. They did not like to show their feelings too much, so they spoke in a short sharp sort of way, leaving much unsaid, as I try to do in this book. Of course, they were usually very brave, and didn't mind dying in battle as long as they could kill some of the enemy as well! They thought this was a good bargain – and these Vikings were great bargainers in everything. They even bargained about whether it was better to pray to Christ or to Odin and Thor, and they were always arguing about which religion was the more *useful* to them. *Horned Helmet* is set about the year 1015, when officially Iceland had been converted for fifteen years; but there were still quite a number of Northmen who were not quite convinced that Christianity was the best religion.

When we talk of the Northern World in the year 1015, we mean not only Norway, Sweden, Denmark, Finland, and Lapland, but also Iceland, Orkney, the Shetlands, the Hebrides, together with parts of Ireland, Scotland, England, Germany, Russia, and even northern France! These Viking Northmen seemed to get everywhere in their longships; and that is the impression I want you to receive from this story. Sometimes, it seems a little confusing, I know – but that is just how it was in those days. You see, one race married another, and then they shared languages, religions, and stories. Why, a year after our story begins, England even borrowed a Danish king – the famous King Canute who is supposed to have tried to turn the waves back!

The helmet in this story is not the sort of Viking helmet with horns on it that one often sees. It is an ancient Celtic helmet like the one that was found in the Thames. At the time of our story, this helmet would be at least a thousand years old – which is one reason why Starkad set such great store by it. It was an 'heirloom', as they used to say then, to be passed on from one to another as long as it lasted. Swords were regarded like that, too. They went on and on for generations, and sometimes, when they broke at last, they were made into spear-heads so that they could carry on the good work a while longer!

The Jomsvikings were a fierce body of seafarers whose home was at Jomsburg, on an island in the Baltic, at the mouth of the river Oder. They were gathered together into a great band by the Danish king, Harald Gormsson, whose nickname was 'Bluetooth'. This King Harald began as a heathen, but after he was converted himself, he tried very hard, and very ferociously, to make all the other Danes Christians. In 988, his son Swein got so tired of Bluetooth's religious frenzy, he organized a revolt and had his father turned out of his kingdom! Then the Jomsvikings fought for Swein instead. They were still foraging about the seas and rivers well into King Canute's reign; sometimes following one leader, sometimes another – and sometimes just pleasing themselves!

Some of them, like Jarl (Earl) Skallagrim, went as far afield as Constantinople, which they called Miklagard, to serve in the Greek Emperor's Varangian Guard and to live among people who followed the teachings of the Greek Orthodox Church. As long as there was a profit in it, they did not mind where in the whole world they went.

A word about Beorn, the boy-hero of this story; his name should really be spelled *Bjorn*, but that looks clumsy, so I have spelled it as it sounds in English.

Incidentally, his silly song about Snorre the Pig is really a sarcastic sneer about an Icelandic chieftain of those times, who often tried to get his own way by force or even treachery. Snorre is described in *Njal's Saga*.

Beorn also tells about another Icelander, Grettir, whom he claims as a relative. In those days, Icelandic families were so intermixed that many folk must have been related to Grettir. This Grettir, whose life-story is told in *Grettir's Saga*, was born in 997, that is, three years before Iceland became partially converted to Christianity, and eighteen years before our story starts. Grettir was a big, strong, rough Icelander who robbed a dead king's burial mound, and who voyaged and fought in many parts of the Northern World.

The incident of the cloak-pin in Chapter 9 is borrowed from *Olaf Tryggvason's Saga*, and it really did happen to two Jomsvikings.

The verse that the priest, Alphege, speaks on page 94 is a translation of *The Dream of the Rood*, written first in Anglo-Saxon by Cynewulf of Northumbria. And the verse spoken by Katla on page 110 comes from another Saxon poem called *The Battle of Maldon*, fought in 991; that is, twenty-four years before our story begins.

Henry Treece

nodding round him, said sharply to Beorn, 'Stop hitting your head against that rock, boy. It will do no good. Your father chose what he wanted to do. It's not your business to complain.'

All the villagers of Thorstead, some of them fisher-folk, some crofter-farmers, grunted and nodded at this, and knocked their axe-heads on the ground to show they agreed with the Old Man.

Beorn was too young to find the right words to answer this. He felt so lonely and sad that he could only go on crying and rubbing his red knuckles into his sore eyes.

The Old Man grew impatient with him. He pulled his brown sheepskin cloak round him and said, 'It is all over. Your father should not have burned down Glam's barn. That is a serious crime, and he knew it. He lived in Iceland long enough to know that. And he need not have jumped over the cliff as he did. Our judgement was simply that he should fight Glam with the axe; and that was fair judgement. Now, as your father has cheated Glam of his payment, you must see to it yourself. You will go with Glam, in payment for his barn, and will be his boy for as long as he wishes. And when he wants you no longer, it is his right to sell you to anyone he pleases. That is the judgement.'

Beorn cried more than ever then. Glam was a big frightening man with yellow teeth and old white scars all over his arms and face. Once he had been a sea-rover in Norway, until he was outlawed for killing the king's nephew after losing a game of chess to him. Glam was a terrible man with the long axe; that was why Beorn's father had jumped over the cliff. He would not have stood a chance. Perhaps he thought it was better to risk what the sea might do to him than what Glam's axe would surely do.

Beorn shouted out, 'My father never burned Glam's barn down, Old Man! It was dry old wood and thatch, and it was the lightning that burned it.'

Glam, standing before the Old Man, threw back his rough head and laughed for all men to hear. 'The lad's a fool,' he said. 'Does anyone think that Thor Thunderer would burn down *my* barn? Well, do they?'

He turned and glared at all the folk. He was such a fierce fighter that they all shook their heads. No one ever disagreed with Glam at Thorstead. So he looked down at Beorn and said, 'You see, boy? All the folk know that I am in the right, and you have heard what Old Man Kol has said – you are mine now, and must do as I say.'

He came forward to take hold of Beorn's hair and lead him away, but the sight of his big red hands was too much. Beorn swung round suddenly and began to race over the grey rocks, and among the stunted heather-bushes and gorse. He heard the folk crying after him, and Glam's heavy feet thudding behind him for a while. Then everything was still, save for the quick thumping of his heart, the never-ending hissing of the sea, and the cracked cry of the sea-birds, who had watched it all and seemed pleased with what they saw.

2 Rock-pool

Beorn lay on the hill under a bleak hawthorn bush that night, cold and hungry, with his teeth chattering and his face wet with tears. Below him, he saw his home, the cabin that his father had built with his own hands, from rocks and turfs and driftwood, its roof of brown reeds from the salt-marsh beyond the headland.

It was a rough enough home, with the draughts coming up under the door, and the cows lowing at the far end of the room; but there had always been a friendly fire burning in the middle of the floor, in the hearth-stones, and good broth bubbling in the iron pot to keep the cold away.

Now that fire had gone out, and no smoke came up through the chimney-hole. But as Beorn watched, another blaze started down at the house. This was Glam's doing. He and his fellows had put a torch to the thatch, and now it flared so brightly that Beorn felt sure the burners would see him watching, under the hawthorn bush. But they were too busy with their work, and went away at last without noticing him.

And when they had gone, Beorn crept down the slope and went among the white ashes of his home, to see if they had left anything at all. He hoped he might find his father's axe, or even his blackthorn staff, anything to remind him; but the men who followed Glam had left nothing that was worth taking. Most of them had been old sea-wolves, and once they swept through a place, there was little left, even for a mouse to eat.

Beorn lay among the warm ashes then and slept till dawn, lightly like a dog. Afterwards he woke and ran into the hills again, for he was not sure when Glam might come back to kick among the ashes in search of plunder he had missed.

In a narrow gully, Beorn knelt down and said a prayer to Father Odin, asking his help. But it seemed no good. A big black raven settled above him on the rock, and watched him steadily with bright eyes until the prayer was finished; then it gave a squawk and flapped away with rattling wings. This was answer enough, thought Beorn. Father Odin's own bird had deserted him, and that was a bad sign.

There were red berries on the whinbushes still, and cold clear water in the streams. Beorn kept himself going on these for a day or two; then, one afternoon, he felt sure that if he could only get down to the shore beyond the headland, he might find meat of some sort, even if it was but a sealskin, with bits of blubber still sticking to it after the men had flayed it. Or perhaps a young whale, washed among the spiky dog-toothed rocks and unable to get afloat again. These creatures were not hard to kill with a stone.

Beorn's mouth watered at the thought of meat, and he was so hungry now that it was the only thing he wanted. Even the thought of his father came second to the hunger that bit at his insides, like a wolf.

So he came down off the hill, keeping behind bushes and rocks and stone walls whenever he could, and hoping that none of the shepherds or village children saw him and raised the alarm-shout. He ran bent double until he was past the settlement, his heart in his mouth. As he drew near Kol's yard, two dogs began to bark furiously, as though a thief had come to steal the goats from the shed. Beorn lay down under the dry-stone wall till old Kol came out and quietened them with a stick, then he scurried on down to the shore.

No men were about, and Beorn was glad of that. Here and there, among the dirty grey pebbles at the water's edge, seaweed fires smouldered, where the women had been flaying seals. A few half-starved dogs prowled about, dodging the incoming waves, looking for scraps of skin or bones. A covey of gulls stood over the blackened carcass of a seal, like old men at a Council Gathering, shaking their red beaks at one another, as though they were passing judgement on some poor comrade. Beorn saw that there was a lame gull, who could only put one foot to the ground, and he thought that this must be the one this Council was trying. He wished he had a stick to chase them away before they passed judgement on the lame gull. Then he thought again, and knew that if he did chase them, or even go to the carcass to see if there was anything left to eat on it, the birds would flap above the shore with such a loud screaming that one of the villagers would be bound to come down and see what was happening. Then they would find him again, and give him to Glam.

So Beorn turned away and scrambled among the rocks, hoping to pick up something in the little pools there. There were anemones, but you couldn't eat them. And heaps of slimy grey-green weed and bladder-wrack. Beorn put some of this into his mouth, then spat it out again because of its bitter taste. It was good enough for burning, when it was dry, but not for eating.

Soon he was so wet and weary, splashing through the rock-pools, that he almost stopped searching for food. It came to him that nothing could be worse than this, not even if he went up to Glam's steading and gave himself up, to take what beating might await him there.

Then, below him, he noticed a basin of rock that was full of mussels. They lay just below the clear water, blue and grey, left by the last tide, just waiting to be scooped up and eaten. Beorn slipped and slithered down the green rocks, his mouth watering so much that he had to swallow hard. Then he was in the pool, and plunging his hands deep into the ice-cold water, already tasting the shellfish in his mind, even before he had broken one open.

He had the first salty fish in his mouth when he heard a rustling sound above him, and turned round quickly. Glam was standing there, his stick of bog-

oak in his right hand, smiling down at him wickedly
and showing his big horse's teeth.

'Eat well, wretch,' Glam said, 'because you'll need
something in your belly to make up for the beating I'm
going to give you for running away.'

Now Beorn could hardly swallow the shellfish. It
stuck in his throat and made him cough and splutter.
He was not hungry any more, only afraid. Glam looked
enormous, on that rock, against the grey sky – like a
troll, with a big shaggy head and rolling eyes.

Beorn said, 'I am sorry, master. I have been so
hungry and frightened. That is why I ran away. I
meant no harm.'

But, all the time he was saying this, he was glancing
one way and the other, to see if there was any chance of
scrambling up the rock at the far side, and getting on to
the headland and away once more.

Crafty Glam knew well enough what was in his
mind, for he laughed and said, 'You may have meant
no harm, dog's son, but I do. My stick, Backbiter, will
teach you a lesson that needs learning, when you do

come up. And do not think to escape me this time. I can run all the way round this little basin and meet you, wherever you turn.'

Beorn cast a quick glance round, and saw that what Glam said was true. The green and slippery slopes of the rock-pool gave him no chance. Glam was bound to get him now.

So he said hoarsely, 'Master Glam, it is no use, I am caught. If my father was here, he would help me against you. But I am alone.'

Glam spat down into the pool and said, 'Your father was a dog, and the son of dogs. Your father was a coward. He would no sooner have faced me today than he did three days ago, when he took the coward's way and flung himself into the sea to avoid my axe.'

This made Beorn angry, and for a while even his fear left him. He knew that his father had once been a brisk fighter, before his sword arm got broken at a boat-launching, and he hated to hear Glam speak so ill of him now. So a plan came into his head, and he said as pitifully as he could, 'You are the strongest man along this shore, master. All the folk fear you. There is nothing I can do now, so please pull me up with your stick, and then I am ready for the thrashing I deserve.'

Glam gave another of his bitter laughs, and said, 'You see sense at last, little dog! I hope you still see sense after I have beaten you. Come up, then.'

Standing at the lip of the rocky basin, he reached down with his staff, so that Beorn could take hold of it. The boy's hands shook so much now that he could hardly take a firm grip on the bog-oak, and twice Glam rapped him hard on the knuckles to liven him up a bit. Beorn did not complain at this, though it was painful enough, for now he saw his chance. Glam had moved on to a part of the rock where the slimy green weed was thickest, so Beorn grasped the staff firmly and, without warning, gave a great tug.

Glam shouted out as his feet slithered from under him, then his heavy body came hurtling down. Beorn sprang away just in time, and heard the man fall into the rock-pool with a splash and an angry groan.

Then the boy was scrambling like a frog back up the slope, terrified in case his feet or hands slipped and let him go tumbling down again beside his enemy.

He gained the top before Glam had got his wind back, and glanced down to see the big man floundering to his feet, drenched through with salt water and stumbling about like a madman, his shoulders and head covered with green weed.

Now that he was out of the basin, Beorn was frightened again at what he had done to Glam. He was sure that the man would follow him the length and breadth of the land to get even with him. In a way, he wished he had gone up and taken his thrashing, then at least he would have known the worst and could have got used to it. For an instant, he even thought of waiting until Glam was on his feet again, and giving in to him just to save being afraid any further. But all at once Glam bellowed out, 'So! Like father, like son! You have brought this on yourself, and no one can save you now! When I have finished with you, even the shore-dogs will not want what I leave!'

Beorn saw the man dragging the flaying-knife from

the hide-belt round his thick waist, and he knew that Glam meant every word he said.

The boy had never been far away from Thorstead before, but he had heard the fishermen talk of Thingvellir, that lay up to the north, in a deep inlet hidden by pine trees. So it came to his thoughts that if he could only get over the headland before Glam caught him, he might somehow struggle on and on; over Eyjafells Glacier and Markar River and even reach Thingvellir, and offer himself as a slave there, if his new master would only keep Glam away from him.

He saw Glam's wet head coming up over the rocky basin and turned and raced towards the headland, bruising his feet and legs against the limpets that clung to the rocks there. At first he got a good start, and hope rose in his heart. But then he knocked his toes against the sharp edge of a rock, and cried out with the sudden pain. Glam's feet came thumping behind him. The man was blowing hard, but was shouting out, 'You can't get away, you little outlaw! I've got you this time!'

Beorn could hardly get his breath now, and the gentle slope that led before him, up to the headland, seemed like a mountain. The gorse spikes tore at his bare legs, and every stone seemed to twist under his feet, as though they were his enemies too. But he was somehow on to the headland, and Glam had not caught him yet, though he was getting closer with each echoing stride.

Beorn knew that, just over the brow of the rocky slope, there was a steep drop of loose shale. If he could only reach that, he could slither down it, full pelt on his backside, and perhaps get down to the far beach.

A hare started up under him, nearly flinging him to the ground, but Beorn skipped over it and ran on. Then he was on to the shale-slope, when suddenly Glam flung his staff and caught him in the middle of the back. It almost winded Beorn, but he did not stop. He saw the bog-oak cudgel go skeltering down the grey slope before him, into some bushes at the bottom, and he thought: At least Glam has lost his stick!

The loose shale fell away before his feet, and Beorn flung himself down, with the dust and dirt flying all over him, into his mouth and eyes and ears. He hurtled onwards and, as he rolled, saw that Glam was only three paces above him, and coming down even faster, because he was so much heavier.

They reached the beach together, and Glam was already grasping out to hold the boy by the hair when a loud voice shouted out, 'What fool's tricks are these? Speak, or by Odin I'll skewer you both!'

Beorn looked up, and then his heart almost jumped out of his chest. A big ship was beached just round the rock, not more than ten paces away, and before it was the tallest man he had ever seen. In his right hand he held a thick-shafted ash-spear as though it were a twig.

3 Man with a Spear

At first, Beorn thought this man must be Thor himself. From his dull iron helmet with the boar's crest, to the gold rings on his fingers, and the decorated swordbelt about his body, he looked a god, or a hero at least. His face was broad, and as brown as a piece of leather. His hair was a rusty red and his eyes as blue as the summer sky. His square beard jutted as stiffly as though it were carved from whalebone. His mighty spear was thrust out in front of him.

What Beorn noticed most, though, was that the iron point of the spear never shook the slightest bit. And it was aimed at Glam's heart now. Glam was twittering like a partridge disturbed on the nest and his voice was not coming out very strongly. He was saying, 'Peace be with you, master. I am only chasing my slave. The little outlaw is trying to run away from a thrashing.'

The red man with the spear said, 'Do you blame him? And who is to give the thrashing?'

Glam answered, 'I am, master. It is my right.'

The man said, 'What have you done, slave, to merit a thrashing from this big fellow?'

Glam tried to answer, raising his voice above Beorn's, but the man with the spear stepped forward a pace and kicked out, sprawling him on the beach. Then the man said to Glam, 'I am a Jomsviking out of Jomsburg in Vendland. My name is Starkad, and, apart from my master, Jarl Skallagrim, no man disobeys when I command. If I say to a seal, "Speak now," then that seal speaks. If I say to a rock, "Dance for me," then the rock dances. Yet you, a stinking hound of a stinking island, dressed in a stinking cowhide that should have gone on to the midden three years ago, you dare to speak first when I am talking to this boy. How do you explain that?'

He bent a little and put the point of his spear against Glam's ribs, just by his heart, and pushed so that the blade went through the horse-hide a little way. Glam lay back so hard on the pebbles that he looked as though he wanted to burrow into the earth. The big man leaned a little more on the ash-spear, and held Glam there.

Beorn was amazed to hear that Glam was crying now, just as he himself had been only a short while before; and this made him even more afraid. For if a man like Glam was crying, then this Jomsviking must be more terrible than any wolf or bear.

Then the man who called himself Starkad said sharply to Beorn, 'Well, I am waiting, slave. What did you do to cause your master so much anger that he comes sliding down the shale-slope like a madman to catch you?'

Beorn noticed that many men, all in iron helmets, and holding spears, were standing by the ship now, and he felt foolish to speak in such brave company. But Starkad was glaring at him with his pale eyes so fearfully that Beorn whispered, 'I am no slave, sir. I am free-born and a farmer's son. This man claims me because my father would not fight him, but jumped over a cliff instead.'

Glam began to cry out, 'His father was a coward. He burned my barn, then he would not face me with the axe.'

Beorn got angry then and began to shout that his father was crippled in the axe-arm, and that, anyway, it was the lightning that had burned Glam's barn. Starkad listened to them both, his features never moving. Only his blue eyes shifted, from one to the other, and his stiff red beard flickered a time or two as the land-breeze caught it.

He said, 'Whether it was lightning or not, if the man died, then that was his punishment, surely?'

Beorn called out.

'This man burned down our house, too, viking. So I have neither father nor house to go to.'

Starkad said coldly, 'It seems that strange bargains are driven in Iceland these days. I have always heard that you Icelanders were wild dogs with a law of your own. To me, it seems that this man has a very good

bargain if he gets a cripple to fling himself over a cliff, then burns that man's house down and takes his son as a slave – all because lightning fired his own barn.'

Glam was yelling out, 'I claim my rights, Joms-viking. I will not let you or anyone, not even Odin, cheat me of my rights.'

When he said this, the Jomsviking's eyes stretched themselves so wide that Beorn thought they would jump out because the lids could not keep them in any longer. It was almost as though Glam had struck the man on the face.

There was an awful quietness then, as the man began to press a little harder on his spear end. Glam started to struggle again and whimper like a trapped fox-cub. Then, from the prow of the longship, a voice called out, 'This fool still speaks of Odin. He is a heathen, then, and does not know that the White-Christ is master in the north today. He does not know the trouble our old king, Harald Bluetooth, once went to, teaching the heathen about the true God.'

Beorn looked past Starkad at the man who spoke from the ship. He was very tall and thin, and had long grey plaits on either side of his head, coming down from below a gilded war-helm. In his bronze-studded belt he carried two swords; one long, one short. In his right hand, a tall ash-spear; on his left arm, a round hide buckler plated with silver strips. His heavy cloak of red wool flared out behind him, like a storm cloud in the setting sun.

The men about the ship, on the shore, began to clap their hands together and shout out, 'Jarl Skallagrim! Jarl Skallagrim!'

Even Starkad seemed rather small beside this splendid man on the ship. And Beorn was scarcely surprised when Glam held out his hands wide and called in a shrill voice, 'I meant no harm, lord. I spoke of Odin only because we poor folk here have always held him as our master. We know no better, lord; we are poor fools, lord. You will see that we mean no harm to the White-Christ, or to old King Bluetooth.'

Jarl Skallagrim smiled like winter, with his grey hair riding the wind about him like a snow cloud. He said bitterly, 'We call at this forsaken midden of a place, to pick up a keg or two of fresh water, and a sheep or two to fill our bellies, voyaging, and we have to listen to a madman who is so afraid to die that he will praise any god or any king in return for his miserable life!'

Starkad called back over his broad shoulder, 'What with him, Jarl? Slave or spear-point?'

Jarl Skallagrim turned his back and began to walk down the deck.

'Neither,' he said, just above the hissing of the sea. 'I want no thing like him aboard *Reindeer*; nor should you want his dog-blood on your point, to eat it away with its poison and blunt it. He is a heathen and that's that. Bind him hand and foot with thongs, and put him into the first rock-pool that will hold him. Not a very deep pool, though. He needs time to think on God before he drowns at the next tide.'

Beorn did not watch while the men did this. Starkad stood looking at him coldly, and said, 'Why do you mourn, boy? He was your enemy.'

Beorn answered, 'I do not like anyone to be hurt, Jomsviking.'

Starkad smiled for the first time and said, 'Then you should have been born into another world than this. Everyone gets hurt, as you should know by now. But why mourn? If this dog keeps howling long enough, someone will come down and take him out of the pool, more's the pity!'

When the other Jomsvikings came back from putting Glam down, and his cries had started echoing along the shore, Starkad turned and began to walk towards the longship, for it was time to catch the ebb-tide and be away.

Beorn was still kneeling among the pebbles when the men strained to push off with the long oars. Now he felt lost indeed. He would almost have been glad to have Glam beside him, for at least that would be some sort of company, bad as it was.

And when the boy had begun to feel that he was shut off from all men, Starkad came to the prow and called to him sharply, 'Well, must we wait here all day for you? Are you afraid to wet your feet and come aboard?'

No dog ever ran to his master as fast as Beorn ran to that ship, gasping as he plunged waist-deep in the cold salt water. Then a black-bearded Jomsviking leaned over the side and hauled him in, grumbling a little that the boy brought so much water into the ship with him.

4 Snorre Pig and the Herring

Reindeer was a vessel of black oak with its planks over-lapping one another, sixty paces from prow to the after-cabin, and twenty paces across the beam. Her dragon-head was cased in thin gold, beaten into the chisel-grooves of the wood. Garnets, as big as a man's thumb-joint, were set in the mask for eyes, and the curling tongue was hammered out of red bronze.

Beorn badly wanted to go up on to the prow-platform and see the dragon-head and touch it, but the watch-out man frowned at him, and he shrank away.

Once they had pulled offshore and *Reindeer* was riding the Iceland Sea like a nutshell, Starkad took the steerboard, and drove the longship like a rider spurring a stallion. He had no eyes for Beorn, but stared ahead.

Jarl Skallagrim only came down amidships, among

the sea-chests, once a day. At other times he was shut in the after-cabin with a man named Thorgaut, trying to learn Latin. It was hard going, for the Jarl was getting over-aged for such things. Often the teacher, who wore wolf-skin and iron byrnie or war-shirt like the rest of the rovers, got angry with him and made him say words over and over again before he was satisfied. The Jarl was very slow at his Latin, though fast enough at spear-play and sword-work. Beorn was glad he didn't have to learn Latin. It made no sense at all to him, as far as he could hear.

There was only one man who would talk to Beorn at first; a man out of Hedeby, called Gauk the Guardian. When Beorn asked why a man should twist his brains at Latin, which was a right dog's tongue, Gauk the Guardian said it was because the word of the White-Christ was set down in Latin; or if that didn't suit you, it could be got at in Greek – but that was worse. It was like trying to read the thorns in a bush.

This Gauk the Guardian was a friendly enough man, who had had a family of his own, in his youth, but they had got lost in a fire when some Franks came up to bring Christ to the Danes by force. Before he joined the viking community at Jomsburg, he had been a butcher. He told Beorn that there wasn't so much difference; they both used axes.

Some of the Jomsvikings got angry with Beorn for running up and down *Reindeer*, especially when they were playing chess and he accidentally knocked their boards sideways. They shouted at him and told him to jump into the sea and swim home to Iceland, where he belonged.

But Gauk took pity on him, and let him help with one of the sheep that they had taken from the hill above the shore. Some of the joints Gauk hung on hide thongs over the side, letting them trail in the water to keep cool and salted for when they were needed. Other pieces were put into buckets of sea-water on deck. The meat the vikings wanted to keep longest was buried in hot ash, in the fire that Gauk lit in a flat iron pan on the after platform. When this was baked a dark brown, Gauk lifted the deck-planks, near the mast-stepping, and put the meat down in the dark there, over the keel, among all the swords and spears. These weapons were thick with pig-fat, to keep them from rusting, so when mutton came up from under-deck, it tasted more like pig-meat than it should have done. But the men were so hungry before they reached Orkney that no one complained.

One night, as they lay under the tent on deck, with the Pole star behind them, Gauk told Beorn that *Reindeer* made a run up to Iceland almost every year, just to see if there was anything worth taking. He said that most of the northland was picked clean now, by one or another, and that if things didn't improve, the Jomsvikings would be running *Reindeer* down the rivers to Miklagard next season, to see if the Greeks had anything they didn't want, in their famous city where the Emperor lived.

Beorn said, 'If you come to Iceland every year, why have I not seen you before?'

Gauk the Guardian laughed and said, 'Because when we come, all the folk go indoors till we have sailed away. Your folk must have kept you under the bed, or in a coffer-chest. That's why you haven't seen us. Folk usually know when we are about; they light bonfires on the hills to tell one another to stay in. Oh, yes, we know all about it! But we pay no heed. In fact, we often find our way by these bonfires at night! In the old days, when vikings were really fierce fellows, ship-men like us would go ashore and burn a whole town down for lighting those bonfires; but not today, now that we know about the White-Christ. Now, we do not even pick slaves up, as often as we used. We mainly take things like cups and swords and money-chests.'

Beorn said, 'When you used to pick slaves up, did you ever take any from Thorstead, master?'

Gauk scratched his head and considered a while. Then he said, 'Oh, aye, only a year or two ago, in a fit of absent-mindedness, we picked up a woman who was down on the shore, gathering weed and driftwood for her fire. She was a pleasant woman, though she wept to leave her husband and her son, and kept us all awake.'

Beorn said then, 'I think that was my mother. Where did you take her, Gauk?'

Gauk wrapped the blanket round him and said, 'God knows, lad. It could have been Norway, or Scotland, or down to Mull. We called at all those places that year, along the route the old Irish monks used to take. It was a bad year for trade; we got hardly enough to keep the bones from poking through our hides.'

Beorn took the man's hand and said, 'Try to remember, Gauk. Where did you set this woman down?'

But Gauk could not remember. He began to get so cross then that Beorn stopped asking, and went to sleep, to dream of his mother, and then his father jumping over the cliff.

One day, when he was feeling more lonely than ever, because the men would not let him run up and down between the sea-chests, and Gauk had cut his finger chopping up a sheep and was lying down brooding, Beorn went to Starkad at the steerboard and said, 'Master, where are we bound for?'

Starkad was like a hound, smelling his direction. He took a long time to bring his eyes down to Beorn.

He said, 'Unless we strike land soon, we are bound for the bottom, like a hundred more that are on the high seas out of sight of land today. Two of the planks on the larboard side need caulking with tar, and that we can't do until we can get ashore. Haven't you heard the water bubbling below decks at night? We're sinking inch by inch, boy. So that's where we are bound for.'

He spoke so calmly that Beorn thought he was joking. But two nights later the water began to come up through the deck and all the men got on to their sea-chests to keep dry. Then Beorn knew that Starkad had meant it.

Jarl Skallagrim stopped working at his Latin and came among the men. He wore a thick frieze jacket now, and a catskin cap, like any other sailor. His fine clothes were put away in his own sea-chest in the after-cabin. If it had not been for his dagger with the gold handle, no one could have told that he was a great sea-lord.

He asked the man at the prow, 'Did you spy land before the dark came on?'

The man shook his head. So Jarl Skallagrim asked Starkad, 'How far have we settled in the last day?'

Starkad said, 'A hand's length, Jarl. One of my hands; they are longer than most other men's.'

Skallagrim smiled and said, 'Then we can expect to keep afloat for two days more, if you don't mind rowing with the water round your necks. There should be land somewhere ahead of us, judging by the stars.'

One of the men said, 'I was in the water, on a skerry off Shetland, for three days, with the salt in one ear and out the other at every turn of the tide. Apart from the gulls that kept standing on my head, it was not so bad.'

Jarl Skallagrim said, 'You must put your leather hat on, Hrut, when we go down this time. It is no pleasure to have birds standing on one's head. Their claws are sharp.'

Then he passed down the longship and ordered a man to fetch up the thick barley-beer from the fore-hold. That night no one slept, with the sea about their ankles, and the beer passing round in an iron helmet for all to share. Gauk saw to it that Beorn drank with the grown men, to keep his heart up. He had never tasted thick barley-beer before. It was sweet and had a honey flavour. Before long he was feeling that he did not much mind about the sea coming into *Reindeer*.

Then Beorn remembered a silly Icelandic song his father used to sing, so he got up on a chest and sang it, without being asked, even.

> *Snorre Pig had a curly tail,*
> *A curly tail, a curly tail,*
> *His head was as round as the top of a pail.*
> *Hey up, for Snorre Pig!*

Snorre Pig had big brown eyes,
Big brown eyes, big brown eyes,
And he was the Jarl of all the sties.
Hey up, for Snorre Pig!

When Snorre Pig met a lady sow,
A lady sow, a lady sow,
He'd smile and bend his knee full low;
Hey up, for Snorre Pig!

But when he met another boar,
Another boar, another boar,
He'd tread him into the farmyard floor;
Hey up, for Snorre Pig!

Beorn sang his song in a clear high voice, with the barley-beer warm in his head, and the sea-wind cold on his cheek; and when he had finished, Jarl Skallagrim said, 'That is what I call poetry! You have no idea what a change it is after all the Latin I have been reading with friend Thorgaut. I like your Snorre Pig, boy, and you shall sing about him every night till *Reindeer* goes down. Pigs are not good things to mention out at sea, I know, but your Snorre is no common pig. Even if he does us no good, I feel that he is such a gentleman he will do us no harm.'

Beorn said, 'Thank you, Jarl. I could sing about him even better if I had a pair of mutton-bone clappers to beat time with.'

Jarl Skallagrim turned to Gauk and said, 'See that the boy has his bone clappers tomorrow.'

Gauk went one better than that, and made a drum for Beorn, of thin sheepskin stretched tight over an old embroidery-frame that he had picked up from somewhere, perhaps Spain, Gauk forgot where. So after that, Beorn sang to the drum, and the men became more friendly to him. Even Starkad smiled at him once – and that was a great deal, for when Starkad smiled a man's head usually fell on to the floor.

And the song must have brought some luck at least, for two days later they sighted a little island off Shetland, and got into a cove there, with the sea up to their waists now, only just in time.

A shipwright named Einar lived there, and he not only caulked the seams with good black pitch and rags; he also told them that the herring had come inshore south along the Scotland-coast, thicker than for ten years.

This made the Jomsvikings so glad that Beorn asked Gauk why. Gauk said, 'When herring come inshore, the coast-folk get excited, and they all go out in their little boats, their cobles and curraghs, and forget to lock their doors, or even leave guards in the villages. So, the thing to do is land a little higher up the coast, and then go overland and take the pickings. Fair's fair – they get the herring; we get the gold! Nothing comes of nothing in this world, lad. A man must pay for what he gets. So, they must pay for the herring.'

After they had this news, and the ship was water-tight, *Reindeer* could hardly wait to be off again. She seemed to know the herring were inshore, and tugged at her mooring like a war-horse that smells iron.

So, two months after they had left Iceland, they stood offshore from a Scottish wick, where they could see the blue smoke rising from the clustered houses of a village, and see the tarred skin-boats, the curraghs, coming out in shoals to drag in the herring.

Starkad allowed himself to say, 'It must have been our lucky day when we found you on the shore, Icelander. I had thoughts of throwing you to the fishes, as we came down through the Ice Sea, but after that pig-song of yours, and now the herring-tidings, I am at the edge of changing my mind, and letting you live. How would that suit you, Icelander?'

Beorn had got more used to this strange man now, and knew when he was jesting, so he smiled and nodded, and even dared to answer, 'That suits me well, Master Starkad, I am in your debt.'

But when he said this, Starkad's face went dark red, and he said angrily, 'Never admit that you are in a man's debt, you donkey! No Jomsviking ever does that. A true man is in no one's debt but his own. Never forget that. All is between himself and God, himself and the king.'

He spoke so furiously that white froth came on to his lips, as though he might fall down in a fit. Beorn had not been so frightened since the day Glam chased him on to the headland.

Beorn said, 'Is that what you mean by saying that he is no ordinary man, Gauk?'

Gauk shook his head, then looked round to see if anyone was listening. Afterwards he bent over Beorn and whispered, 'Starkad is *one of them*, boy.'

He looked so wise when he said this, that Beorn was more puzzled than ever. '*One of them?*' he said. 'What does that mean, Gauk?'

Gauk made a strange face, then said, 'God above, but you *must* be an Outlander, not to know! Then I will tell you in plain words, since you are so dull – Starkad is a baresark. That's what. When the froth comes on to his mouth, as you have just seen it, he is already at the first stage. The next stage is when he rips off his war-shirt, his byrnie. The third stage is when he begins to roll his eyes round and bite at things. And the last stage is when he screams out and runs at whoever gets in the way. That is a baresark. You used to have them in Iceland. It is a terrible thing to be, but there it is; a man does not ask for it. God sends it, just as He sends thunder and lightning. So now you know.'

Then Beorn understood why all the men looked up to Starkad, and why, when Starkad spoke, even Jarl Skallagrim was silent. For a baresark was not bound by the rules that other men must obey; he was his own rule. To be a baresark was like being born a Jarl, or even a King. And when it ran in families, so that all the men-folk were baresarks, that was the most frightful thing of all, for such a family was almost holy. Ordinary folk laid offerings at their door, and no baresark ever had to do common work, like milking a cow, cutting turf, or ploughing a field. There was a saying among the folk of Hedeby at this time: 'Better a burgher than a beggar; but better a baresark far!'

After this, whenever Starkad spoke to Beorn, the boy felt that he was listening to words from the Other World, where thunderbolts were forged in the fire, and lightning was hammered bright by Thor.

That night, while the herring-smacks were out, the Jomsvikings hauled down their striped sail and folded it carefully. They unstepped the mast as well, and laid it on deck, so that they should not be seen from the high village. Then every man put on a grey cloak and hood, over his helmet and mesh-byrnie, so that moonlight should not glint on them. When they rowed inshore, they wrapped old sheepskins round the oarblades so that the water should not clap on to the ashwood and make a noise, to give warning of their coming.

Gauk lent Beorn a little cloak and hood, and found a black-oak sea-spike for him to carry like a sword. Though, to tell the truth, Beorn had little enough wish to go ashore hurting anyone at that time; he was still too full of remembering how his father had been hurt, and even how bad Glam had been tied up in the rockpool for the sea to smother, unless someone saved him before the tide came in.

But after they had pulled *Reindeer* up into a little stream, and covered her over with gorse and saltgrasses, Beorn felt himself getting more and more excited. He told himself that he would just go ashore with the Jomsvikings, but would take care not to hurt anyone.

Gauk took him aside and said quietly, 'Keep out of

Starkad's way, lad. The froth is on his lips again. Once he sees the thatch burning, he will not know whether you are fish, fowl, or good red herring. Give him best, as the others do. There must be a clear space round him, or we'll be short of a crew tomorrow.'

The boy answered, 'I will keep by you, then, Gauk.'

But Gauk shook his head. 'Nay, lad, that you must not do, for my place is close to Starkad. I go three paces behind him, to guard his back. That is why they call me the Guardian. I am Starkad's Guardian, the eyes in his back, to keep anyone coming at him from behind while he is at work.'

Beorn had often heard the shipmen calling Gauk 'Guardian', but he had thought little of it at the time. Indeed, he had thought they meant that Gauk looked after the butcher's meat on the voyage, no more. Now this was answered in his mind and suddenly he turned and said, 'And are you a baresark, too, friend?'

But Gauk the Guardian smiled and shook his head. 'Only half-way there,' he answered. 'And that is just as well, for two baresarks together do not last very long. They only face one way, and each tries to outdo the other. That is when they fall – when their pride blinds them and they cannot see the wood for the trees.'

Beorn gazed up at him and said, 'You talk like a woodcutter, not a Jomsviking, Gauk the Guardian!'

The man laughed and said, 'What we chop down are no trees, little one. But my meaning was that a baresark will run among hosts of men, though they be as thick-planted as a forest around him. That is when he ends, when there are trees behind him as well as in front of him. Now you understand?'

Beorn nodded, sadly, and while the Jomsvikings were drinking a horn of strong ale before climbing up to the village, Gauk put him in the care of Thorgaut the scholar, and Odd, a sea-wolf with a great hooked nose, and a hunched back which he had got from falling out of a tree when he was a boy, searching for owls' nests.

These two were to go in the rear of the attack, for they were not as nimble as the others, though they were as brisk as most warriors who were not Jomsvikings.

At last, when torches flared out from the fishing-boats among the herring shoals, and men's loud voices came up the cliff as the laden nets were drawn in, Jarl Skallagrim passed the word round that the time had come. The men tied strips of sheepskin round their feet and set off in a long line, up among the gorse and the tussocky grass.

Beorn's heart thumped so hard, he thought everyone would hear, but no one mentioned it. No one spoke at all. The whole shipload of men moved like ghosts in the dark, silently. Only when they stood on a mound, an arrow's flight from the lighted village, did Thorgaut whisper, 'Stay between Odd and me, my boy. Do not go off on your own.' He had no need to say this, for now Beorn was far too frightened to leave them.

There was no stockade round the cluster of stone huts, for this was a village of fishermen, not herdsmen. The highest building was a wooden hall of black oak, with a steep thatched roof.

Odd pointed with his axe and whispered, 'Their chief's house. There the treasure will be. There Starkad and Skallagrim will be found at the fighting's sunset.'

Beorn's legs were trembling as though he had run a mile. His fingers lost their use and he dropped his cudgel in the darkness and did not even bother to search for it. He was so afraid. But, when the battle-run started, he forgot his fear and dashed in and out of the houses yelling like everyone else – though he hardly knew what he was yelling about.

Most of the fishermen were down on the sea in the black curraghs, so the Jomsvikings had small work for their axes. The women and old men who sat by their hearth-fires were too surprised to do much, and stared, on their knees, their lips praying, while the sea-rovers snatched up what they could find.

Only once did a tall girl with long yellow plaits come storming out, swinging a heavy ladle as though she was a Valkyr with an axe. She almost knocked Thorgaut senseless with it, and Odd had to hit her on the head with his ash-shaft: just hard enough, and no more. Then he smiled and said, 'A real shield-maiden, that, Beorn. If I ever married, that is the sort of woman I would pick. I did not think they bred them so, outside Jomsburg!'

All told, it was no great fight, and the Jomsvikings were soon loaded with as much as they could carry. Beorn was glad it was over and was ready to turn and go back to *Reindeer*, with others who were trooping off with their pickings, down the cliff-path.

But something happened which kept him, and changed the whole of his life to come.

A man called Dag, whose job it was always to fold *Reindeer*'s sail properly, came staggering past with an iron-bound chest and, seeing Thorgaut and Odd, shook his head and said, 'Oh, a fine carry-on! We'll be here till dawn and the Scottishmen come up from the fishing. The Jarl is off his head, I can tell you!'

Odd asked, 'What is it? Are some of our fellows hurt?'

Dag shook his head. 'Nay,' he said, 'it's Starkad again. He's in their chief's house and won't come away. No one can shift him; he's beyond caring.'

Thorgaut said gravely, 'This is what comes of sailing with baresarks. They can put a whole shipload in danger at times like this.'

He began to stride forward. Dag called after him, 'A fat lot of good you will do, shipmate. He's already knocked Gauk down twice, and the Jarl once!'

Then he stumbled off with his treasure-chest into the dark. Beorn had to run, to keep up with Odd and Thorgaut.

6 Lost Sword and Found Son

Inside the chief's hall, with the torches blazing and the round bucklers ranged on the walls, Beorn saw a strange sight. Gauk and Jarl Skallagrim were sitting on the floor, rubbing their heads like men just waking: Starkad staggered about, waving his arms, stumbling over the bodies of five men, guards, to judge by their helmets and byrnies, who lay huddled about a great coffer.

Beorn saw that the coffer-lid had been split across and wrecked, and that the box was full to the brim with cups and coins that glimmered in the flickering light.

Starkad was staring about him with empty, wide-open eyes, that looked more like pieces of flint or agate than anything else. He was saying, 'My dear sword has gone. Leg-biter has gone! He belonged to my grand-father and in all those years his edge was never hacked. Oh, Leg-biter, oh dear friend! What is this rubbish worth if you have gone?'

Then Starkad began to kick out at the treasure chest, making the broken lid rattle, and spilling coins out among the rushes on the floor.

Gauk saw Thorgaut and said, 'He broke his sword hacking open the lid, after he had put paid to three of those poor fellows down there. Now he won't come away. Do you think you could help to carry him?'

Thorgaut said, 'I would as soon try to carry a she-bear away from her cubs, friend!'

Starkad must have heard this, for he swung round and shouted, 'Who else wishes to lie here? I still have the hilt of Leg-biter, and that is enough for most men I know.'

The four Jomsvikings stood like stone as Starkad came down the hall towards them. Beorn noticed that even Jarl Skallagrim's hands were trembling.

When Starkad was three paces from them, he stopped and said, 'Well, which of you is to be the first? Take your pick. It is all one to me.'

In the sudden silence that followed, Beorn heard himself say, 'I will come to you, Starkad. You came to me, when I needed you, on the Iceland shore. You saved me from Glam, Starkad. So I will save you.'

Beorn felt his feet moving as though they belonged to someone else. He heard Gauk draw in his breath sharply, behind him, like a man plunging into icy water off a cliff. Then he saw Starkad bending down to-wards him, his fierce face growing bigger and bigger, his hands reaching out with hooked fingers, like a goshawk's talons.

The next thing Beorn knew, he was swung up into the air – and then he was sitting astride Starkad's shoulders, and Starkad was laughing as though someone had told him the funniest story in the world.

'Oh, boy, boy, boy!' the baresark was saying. 'I have lost a sword and found a hero! I have found another swordless one who dares stand against me, though he is no taller than a sword himself!'

The empty look had gone from Starkad's eyes, and he was prancing like a war-horse. Beorn was beginning to tremble and was wondering whether he might be sick with all this jolting up and down. He felt cold all over as he held on to Starkad's thick hair to keep himself from tumbling.

And now, strangely, the Jarl and the others were all smiling, with their swords and axes put away, and Starkad was still calling out, 'Tonight I am as happy as a spring lark. I am as brisk as a bridegroom. I am as free as a young stallion who first sniffs the mountain wind.'

Beorn heard Gauk say to the Jarl, 'All is well. The fit has passed, praise be to God. Now we can take the treasure-chest and go down to the ship.'

But Starkad was already dancing out of the door, and off through the darkness towards the cliff-path. He did not stumble once, although Beorn, who had no great head for heights, was often afraid he might.

Reindeer put off again just as dawn was breaking and the fishing-curraghs were pulling in with their catch. All the Jomsvikings were well pleased with their

night's work, and lay about the deck in the morning sunshine, while Dag unfurled the sail and let the wind belly into it and swing them out to sea.

Beorn was so tired, he could have slept on the yard-arm. Gauk had put a sheepskin down for him, under the prow platform, out of the spray. But just as he was about to lie down, Starkad came forward and raised him up again, smiling and patting his shoulder with his great hard hand.

'Come, Beorn,' the baresark was saying. 'I cannot find a shipmate and lose him, all in one night. From this time, lad, you shall share my sleeping-place and be like a son to me. And you shall sing your Snorre Pig song only for me, and for no other. And what I gain shall be half yours. And I will stand by you against all the world.'

Beorn went with him, almost weeping now for happiness.

7 Grettir's Venture

Starkad was a changed man after that night at the village on the cliff. As *Reindeer* ran southwards, with the grey Scotland-coast just in sight, he would even let Beorn take the steerboard-shaft, if the going was clear and the tide light. This was a thing he had never let another man do; it was like lending a man your horse, or your sword – to lend such things was always a risk, for a horse could break a leg and a sword-edge be hacked. Beorn felt very proud; but he was always glad when Starkad took the steering back again, for *Reindeer*, though she danced lightly enough on the wave-tops, was wayward to handle, being so broad in the beam. What is more, she seemed to know when Beorn had the guiding of her, for she would tug so hard that the boy feared she might turn about and set off back to the north!

Starkad used to smile and say, 'These ships are like women. All sweetness and gentleness, when they are tamed. But it is the taming that counts, and that calls for a firm man.'

Once he said, 'I had a wife once, a pretty dark girl from Syria. That was when I fought for the old Emperor at Miklagard, among the Varangers, his viking guard.'

Beorn's eyes went wide at this, for he thought that all Northmen who had been to Constantinople, the City of Gold, were the next best to being magic men. 'Tell me, what was it like?' he asked.

A far-away look was in Starkad's eye. He said, 'I was a young fellow then, and I have almost forgotten. I know it was a terrible, cold run, down the rivers and over the Great Portage. We had to roll the longship on tree-trunks from river to river, and many of us died, with the strain and the cold, and sometimes the wolf-packs. But we got there in the end. We never thought we should, because of the Patzinaks.'

Beorn said, in wonder, 'What are they, the Patzinaks, Starkad?'

Starkad smiled and said, 'A sort of dwarf, or troll, I think. They live down there, on the plains in the howling wind, among the marshes and the tall grasses. They never walk, but always ride on little ponies that understand every word they say to them. You have never seen such folk, lad. Their faces are as yellow as my pigskin belt, and their eyes are like little black stones glimmering through slits in their skin. I tell you, to see them hunched up on their sheepskin saddles, with their high hats and their little horn-bows that can drive a shaft through a bullock, is no pleasant sight.'

Beorn said, 'Tell me, what did they do to you, Starkad?'

The man shrugged his shoulders and said, 'At first they used to ride down the river bank as we pulled at the oars, and see how many of us they could pick off with their arrows. They thought we had come to dig their old kings up, from the burial place near the Big Waterfall. But when they found we were set for the south to join the Emperor's Guard, they stopped shooting. Or perhaps it was something to do with what happened the night we got tired of them and went ashore with the axes. Jarl Skallagrim took ten heads and hung them on the prow. Aye, I've known him when no man could stand before him, for all his quietness and his Latin, lad! That night, we followed the Patzinaks and burned two of their tent-villages. After that, they passed the word on, with little fires, and the other horsemen, down along the far plains, treated us well. They would call us ashore to eat out of their big iron kettles, and even give us some of their scrawny sheep to take on board for food. These Patzinaks grew no hair on their faces, and our beards were a marvel to them. I got so weary at them fingering mine, I chopped it short. I gave one of their chiefs the end-cuttings, and he danced about as though I had awarded him the Treasure of Asgard, he was so pleased.'

Starkad stopped then, and lifted the short plank near the steerboard. From the darkness under the plank, he hauled up his sailing bag, made of a sheepskin, with the greasy fleece on the inside to keep things from rusting in the damp below-decks. He rummaged for a space, among his treasures, then pulled out an iron image of a stag kneeling, with the points of its antlers spraying out like a fountain.

He put it in Beorn's hand. 'This is what he gave me in return for my beard,' he said. 'It is very old. A scholar I spoke with once, in Frankland, told me that an old Scythian must have hammered and chiselled this stag, generations before even the Romans came.'

Beorn gazed at the stag with wonder. There was a strange glint on the iron, almost as though it had a brown enamel over it, but there were blues and even reds in the glint as well. He said, 'I have never seen anything so lovely, Starkad. This must be a magic thing.'

Starkad shrugged his shoulders and put on a weary look. 'I have carried it in my bag ever since,' he said, 'and I do not know that it has brought me good luck or ill. Now, with a sword, it is different. A sword can rule a man's life entirely – but not a stag. Keep it for yourself, Beorn. It has travelled farther afield than most men, and is older than any man. You shall have it.'

When Beorn said that he couldn't take such a splendid thing, Starkad looked over the sea and answered, 'Then I shall throw it overboard. If it is not fit for an Iceland boy to accept, it is not fit for Starkad to carry about any longer.'

Beorn knew that he was serious now. So he took the iron stag and swore that he would never part with it for the rest of his life.

Starkad laughed at this and said, 'Don't hold to the

stag too hard, lad. One day you might be glad to swap it for a loaf of bread.'

'No, I never shall, Starkad,' said Beorn, with tears in his eyes, for no one had ever given him anything like this before.

Starkad drew the boy to him and wiped the tears away with the hem of his woollen shirt. 'What, crying because I give you a stag?' he said. 'That's no way for a sea-rover. Come, take the steerboard again. That will keep you too busy to cry!'

And it did!

Another time as they sailed on Beorn asked what Miklagard was like. Starkad said that it was well enough, with its towers and walls and big streets. But there were too many churches, he said, and too much praying. There were too many princes and princesses as well; a viking Varanger in the Emperor's Guard had to remember so many names, titles, and the proper ways of speaking to each of the princes, it was often a relief to get out into the hills and fight one of the Bulgar tribes, savage though they were.

Starkad only mentioned his wife once; he said her name was Maria Anastasia, and she could play the lute better than anyone he had ever heard since. No more than that. Beorn asked where she was now, and Starkad said, 'Oh, it was the plague they have down there in the summer. She dropped her lute and died. We had a son, called Constantine. He took the plague, too, and went with her. He would have been about your age now, but his hair was black.'

Then Starkad went on and told what it was like in Palestine and Egypt and Sicily. He never spoke of

Anastasia and Constantine again, but often he would put his arm round Beorn and give him a bear-hug for no reason at all.

One day, as they lay ashore waiting for Odd and Thorgaut and Dag to bring a few sheep down from a hillside, Starkad said, 'I feel at a loss, without a sword, Beorn. I can manage with the axe, but it is not my weapon. If we ever get down to Northumbria, I must look out for a new sword. Did I ever sing the old Widow Song for you?'

Beorn shook his head; Starkad often used to break off like that, and the only thing was to let him ramble on till he was done.

Now he sang:

> *Makers of widows, wander we must,*
> *Killers 'twixt seedtime and salting of kine,*
> *Walking the Whale's Way, sailing the Swan's Path,*
> *Daring the Sun's Track, tricking dark death!*
>
> *In the jaws of the storm, jesting we stand,*
> *Lashed with hail's fury, hands frozen to line;*
> *Numb head rain-shaken, sharp spume in the nostril,*
> *Salt caking hair – and blood's haven in sight!*

When he got to the end of the song, he gave such a hard thump on the gunwale beside him that Beorn nearly jumped in the air.

Starkad saw this and laughed. 'Aye, that was the old rowing-song,' he said. 'It kept the oars going in time, and the folk who heard it, up on the shore, got to know it! After they had heard it, we never had much trouble sailing in and taking what we needed. But the old days are going fast, lad, and I'll wager you there are not more than a hundred men in the world who could still sing you that song.'

Beorn thought a while, then said, 'Up in Iceland the old men say the same. They say the world is growing old and tired and is almost ready to end. They say that on the day all men take Christ as their lord, the world will sink into the sea.'

Starkad nodded. 'There may be something in that,' he said, 'for I have noticed that whenever a folk take the priests as their law-givers, they all get to be so gentle that it's almost a shame to rob them. They are like women. Thank God we are only half-Christians!'

Beorn said, 'It will be a fair while before the Icelanders get like that, Starkad. News reaches them slowly. Did you ever hear of my father's kinsman, Grettir? He swore an oath to keep the old ways living, and went round the north burning houses and finding trolls to kill. I never saw him, he had gone to Norway before I was big enough to remember him, but my father often told me of the things he got up to. Some of them were terrible.'

Starkad was whittling a piece of wood with a knife, and said, 'Tell me some of them. I like to hear of a man with principles.'

Beorn scratched his head, then said, 'Well, he once killed an alderman with a milking stool, and got outlawed.'

Starkad nodded and tossed the stick over the side. 'That is well enough,' he said, 'but I wouldn't say it was the bravest thing I had heard of – though Grettir was your kinsman.'

The boy thought again, and suddenly said, 'Oh, there was a time when he really did something great. It was at Haramsey, at Thorfinn's Steading. There was a dead old king there, named Karr, who lay in a dark mound, a burial howe, with all his brooches and weapons. So my kinsman went out one night, dug the mound open, and let himself down with a rope.'

Starkad turned to him with a serious face and said, 'What then, Beorn? This is really to my taste.'

Beorn said, 'Well, it was awful, because as soon as Grettir had found himself a sword and was coming away, the dead king jumped to life and started wrestling with him, trying to break his neck.'

Starkad leaned forward and took the boy's hands strongly. 'Go on, go on!' he said. 'Why have you never told me this before?'

Beorn said, 'You never asked me. Well, all I can say is that Grettir side-stepped old King Karr, then cut off his head and laid it beside his thigh, in the proper manner, to stop the ghost from getting up again.'

'What of the sword, though?' said Starkad, his pale eyes glaring. 'Did it bring him luck?'

Beorn said, 'As far as I know, it did. He used it on a good few baresarks to his advantage before we lost track of him.'

Starkad got up and went roaming along the deck, his hand tugging at his stubbly beard. All the men got out of his way. At last he came back and sat down again by Beorn. 'I am glad you told me this,' he said. 'Now I am certain that you bring good fortune with you. It was in my mind to go to a swordsmith in Deira, one day soon, and *buy* myself a new sword, like any ordinary fellow.

But now I see the right thing to do. A man such as I am should not buy a sword, for a bought sword carries no virtue in its edge. The correct thing would be to take one from a burial howe, then I should be sure that it was an heirloom and carried the old magic in its blade. These new blades have no more magic in them than a hedge-knife, or a bill-hook such as thralls use on the farms.'

Jarl Skallagrim had come up and was listening to this. He said, 'You would be wiser to buy yourself a sword, axe-friend. Most of the howes are broken open by now, and the best weapons are all gone.'

Starkad glared at him so hard then that the Jarl said, 'Very well, a man must make up his own mind, I see. If you want to do what this lad's kinsman did, then I know a place down the coast, three days away, where there is a howe or two. But they lie close to a village where the men are as wild as wolves. That is why they have never been robbed before; most sea-rovers give them a wide berth, for it is a bad bargain to raid such a place and go back to the boat with half the rowers dead.'

Starkad said, 'We will worry about that when the time comes. You point out this place to me, friend, and I will do the rest. Now tell me as much as you can remember, Beorn, about how Grettir did this deed.'

8 Dead Man's Howe

At last *Reindeer* came down to Howestead, and, with the autumn turning towards winter and fetching the grey skies out to hide the sun, a more desolate place was not to be seen anywhere in the north.

Skallagrim said, 'I do not like the look of this steading, friend Starkad. It has all the looks of a place where a man might find his doom waiting. I counsel you, I who have given you rings and war-gear in the past as a lord should, not to go there. Look, I will give you a sword from my store. I have four of them, stowed under-decks, and you shall take your pick. How is that?'

Starkad gave a wrench at the steerboard-shaft and said, 'Jarl, I follow you in all things – but in this matter of getting a new sword, I must be governed by my heart. And heart says that my sword rests up there, beyond the steading. I have spoken. There is no more to say.'

Beorn and the others stared towards the land, where, on the high grey cliff-edge, the tumble-down huts clustered, like rugged clams on a rock. To Beorn, the huts looked more like wild beasts crouching than dwelling-places. It was late afternoon and brown smoke rose above the place, eddying in the light air, like a dirty blanket. Up there, they were weed-burners, he thought. He had seen smoke like that in Iceland, and knew that the men of Howestead must be busy at other trades than gathering wood, if they burned shore-weed. He wondered what their business was.

Skallagrim turned to Gauk and said, 'Shipmate, what is your opinion? You are a man of good sense, can you not persuade Starkad to get his sword another way?'

Gauk scratched the end of his pointed red nose and said, 'Jarl, my advice is not worth a horse's cast shoe, for my sense comes and goes, like any other man's. So do not ask me that. All I can tell you is that I was sworn in as Starkad's Guardian, and so, whatever he chooses to do, I am bound to follow at his back.'

Skallagrim said, 'I bound you by that oath, and I can release you from it. Now, say what is in your mind, without fear or favour.'

Gauk said, 'Then look you, Master Jarl; if I had sworn to follow you to the world's edge where the mermaids play and the sea-horses snort on the waters, you would expect me to go with you, would you not?'

Skallagrim nodded. 'That is the law,' he said.

'Very well,' said Gauk. 'Now if a man came and offered to take my oath from me, would you not feel betrayed?'

The Jarl turned away and said, 'Very well. What must be, must. But look at the rock which lies off their shore and see if you call it a good sign.'

They looked. It was the tallest column of rock Beorn had ever seen, and reached upward like the end of a blunt sword, into the grey sky, olive-green and dusty brown, with sheer sides, and, here and there, narrow ledges covered with dry heather. On one ledge, a little wider than the rest, half-way down the pillar, a heap of bones lay silent and white.

Beorn said to Gauk, 'How did they get up there, friend?'

Gauk made little of it. He said, 'Maybe the Homestead folk sacrifice to this rock and lay the offerings there. Or maybe these are the bones of silly goats that once climbed up and could never get down again.'

Jarl Skallagrim came between them both and said, 'Well you may ask, lad. Aye, well you may ask. Now look again, and see the cormorants, the black-backed gulls, and, at the highest tip, even the hawks, sitting still, waiting on that rock. And, look, on the landward side there is a family of seals, rolling in the lee, not foraging as they mostly do. That is a bad sign, for seals are stupid folk and will go anywhere to pick up scraps. But these seals know better than to go inshore, and it is my counsel that where seals will not go, vikings should not.'

Starkad smiled and said, 'Master, I have sailed with

you since I was a boy with no hair on my face. Have you ever known me go against your wish before?'

The Jarl said, 'Have it as you will. But, one thing, Starkad, I have a whole ship's company in my care, whose widows must be paid blood-money if they are lost. *Reindeer* is no small prize, either, and would buy me a palace in Novgorod. So, I am forced to tell you this: I cannot risk ship or men on this venture for a mere sword. I will set you ashore tonight and will wait for you a reasonable space. Then, when the time is up, I will sound three long blasts on the horn and that will mean we must be away. If you do not come after a count of three hundred, said slowly, then I must put off to sea again. Now are you set on going?'

Starkad smiled and nodded, 'Jarl,' he said, 'when have you known me turn my hand away from work I have begun?'

Jarl Skallagrim grunted angrily and said, 'Truly are you called a baresark. Where there is no sense, there is no reason. But never forget, my friend, that I asked you not to go.'

Beorn felt sorry for the Jarl, for he could see that the man loved Starkad; but then the boy's heart almost stopped, for Starkad said, 'I shall not forget, master. I shall not need to, for I shall come back with the sword, never fear. And, so that my luck holds, let me take the boy with me. He put the notion into my head, so it must be in the heart of Odin that he should come and help me get the sword.'

Jarl Skallagrim was so angry then that he clenched his fist as though he meant to hit someone. 'What do you say to that, Beorn?' he asked, when he could speak.

Beorn was like a man between two horses, being pulled two ways at once. He truly believed what the Jarl had said about this place – but in his hand he still held that lovely iron stag that Starkad had given him. And it ill became a man to desert a comrade.

Beorn said, at last, 'I will go with Starkad, Jarl.'

Starkad did not seem to hear him, but Gauk patted him on the shoulder and whispered, 'Well said, warrior. A man can die only once, after all.'

So, that night, when the moon was behind a cloud, the three of them were put ashore, and waded, waist-deep, through the shallows towards Howestead cliffs.

The burial mounds were not hard to find, even in the dim moonlight, for they stood like three domes, each higher than a king's house, above the village on the landward side. Starkad stopped by the tallest of them. 'This,' he said, 'is where the best swords should be, friends.'

They clambered silently to the top, keeping on the far side away from the torchlit houses, and then Starkad and Gauk began to dig furiously with wooden mattocks, while Beorn kept watch.

The earth on the mound was thin, for wind had blown it away and rain had punished it, since that howe was made. No turf grew on it, to make the digging harder with its tangled roots. Soon Starkad's mattock hit hard on a wood baulk.

He said softly, 'We are at the roof already, friends!'

Though he whispered, Beorn could hear the trembling joy in his voice, deep in his throat. Then Starkad and Gauk went at the timbers like wolves scratching a cottage door in winter. And soon they began to grunt and groan as they hoisted up a gnarled oak timber; then another; then another.

Gauk stood back and said, 'Pah! the air down there has not been breathed for a hundred years. You could slice it with a knife.'

Starkad laughed quietly and answered, 'It is a sword, not air, that we come for, Guardian. Come, tie the rope round me and let me down. I must do the best I can in the dark, for we dare not strike flint on iron and light a torch, or they would see us from the steading.'

So Starkad went down into the howe, with Gauk and Beorn holding hard on the plaited hide rope above. It was not easy, for Starkad was a heavy man and began to swing this way and that, once four yards of rope had been paid out. Beorn was afraid that he might be dragged into that musty dark hole himself, into the place where the dead king lay. Not even for Starkad would he have gone down there. Not even for that iron stag.

But at last the rope went slack, and Gauk whispered, 'He has reached the ground. Now we must rest, for it will be twice as hard to get him up again, lad.'

Beorn lay on the howe-top, shivering in the night breeze, and trying to listen for any sound of struggle down below. He remembered Grettir wrestling with his dead king, and expected to hear shouting and the thud of blows at any minute. But all he heard was an owl crying in the distance, and a muffled curse from Starkad, as though he had barked his shins on something in the dark.

At last there came a tug on the rope, and Starkad's voice saying, 'Hoist me up! I've got what I came for, and more!'

Truly, it was hard-pulling to get him back again, but they did it, and Starkad helped them by setting his feet on the howe side whenever he could, and using his legs as a lever. The moonlight gave them benefit once he was out, and they saw that his journey into the darkness had been repaid. Under his arm he carried two swords – one a gold-hilted beauty in a calfskin scabbard decorated at the end with a silver chape; the other a short sax, single-edged, but as light as an alder stick in the hand, and as whippy, too.

He handed this to Beorn. 'Here, lad,' he said, 'it is time you had a blade of your own. Do not refuse: you helped as much as any. Now you can always brag you robbed a king's howe, like your kinsman from Iceland!'

He turned to Gauk then and held out a helmet towards him. 'You have a sword, friend,' he said, 'but I've noticed lately that your old war-helm has seen better days, and needs replacing before a sword finds its weak spot and sends you home!'

Gauk was as pleased as Beorn with the gift, for the helmet was unlike anything he had seen before. It was all of bronze, and two horns stood out straight from its sides, covered with fine chiselling and moulding, of oak-leaves and hunting-dogs. He set it on his head and it was as though the smith had made it for him.

Starkad said, 'It is hard to tell, in this dim light, but I would guess that the man who made that had a sharp word or two to say to the Romans when they came here first. It is very old, and a bit green with bronze-rust, but a rub or two with a rag will get it clean again.'

The two were speechless. 'Come,' said Starkad, 'a gift for a gift, that is the law. We have taken the dead king's gear, so fling our rope down into the dark for him – and the debt is paid.'

This Gauk did, although he hated losing that rope. It had been his father's and was made of ten reindeer hides, got from a tent-steading in Lappland. But he did it, because what they had got from the howe that night was beyond price.

He whispered, 'Starkad, if I were a skald, I would make a great gay song, I am so happy.'

Beorn whispered also, 'If we were clear of this place, I would sing the song about the pig, with all my heart.'

Starkad said, 'Both of you can wait till we are back aboard, then I will join you in a song – and I promise you, it will be such a song as no man has ever heard before. They will think we are mad, I can tell you, but little shall we care!'

But, as the three of them turned to slither down the howe, a harsh voice came up at them from below and said, 'There is no need to whisper any more, grave-thieves. You will not rouse the village, for the village is already waiting for you, and has been, for the past hour.'

They looked down and, as the moon came from behind a cloud, they saw a hundred men with spears about the howe, standing in silence.

Starkad turned and laughed to Gauk. 'The Jarl was right,' he said. 'His mother must have been a Finland witch! Well, we will go down the howe fighting. Lend

Gauk your sword, Beorn, and keep between us. If we get a good run on, we can break through this flock of sheep, and it's hardly more than half a mile to the ship. These fat cattle will never catch us, once we are away.'

But that run was never even started, for a shower of rocks came up at them from the darkness below, tumbling them to the ground.

9 Two Vikings and a Log

Beorn felt himself being carried along roughly, like a captured bear on a stick. Distantly he heard the three blasts on the horn, as Jarl Skallagrim had promised; then he lost his senses again.

It was dawn when he woke. He was sitting on the ground in a cleared space between the grey huts of Howestead, and his feet were lashed to a long thick oak-log. On one side of him sat Starkad, and on the other, Gauk. They were both rubbing their eyes, and groaning when they touched their heads where the stones had struck. But, worn as they were, and weary, they were laughing. Starkad said, 'We thought you would never wake, Beorn! What a thing it is to be young and carefree!'

On the other side of the oak trunk Beorn could see the two swords and the horned helmet, lying together, as though they were witnesses of the theft. He said, 'Jarl Skallagrim will have gone with *Reindeer*, now, Starkad. What shall we do?'

Starkad said, 'Never think that you are the first to ask yourself that question, lad. Gauk and I have been chewing it over for an hour, while you were snoring your head off in your warm bed!'

Gauk said, 'Do not worry, Beorn lad. I have a feeling that we shall go on many journeys together after all this is over. Look, when their headman comes, I will talk to him and make him see sense. We will give back what we have stolen, and a few other things besides, and so all will be well.'

But Beorn was not sure of this, and, as it turned out, he was right. For an hour later, when the sun was up and about, warming the ground, the headman came out with ten spearmen and a big fellow carrying a double-handed axe. The headman stood beside the helmet and swords and said, 'This is a bad business, wanderers. Little joy lies in putting an end to such as you, but what is a man to do if he wants to keep the respect of his folk?'

Gauk answered, 'From your speech, headman, you are a Danishman, out of Roeskilde, I would guess. And we are vikings out of Jomsburg – so, it is like a family gathering, no more.'

The headman put on a sorrowful face and said, 'You and I are Danishmen, true enough, but my folk here are not. They are stubborn Caledonians, and will not forgive you for stripping their old king.'

Starkad laughed and said, 'Come, come, friend, we did not strip him! He still wears his byrnie and leggings. We only took what you see. Why, we even left him his spear and his buckler. I could have brought those up, too.'

The headman said, 'Little good would it have done you, Jomsviking. They would have lain before you now as witnesses, just as the swords and helmet do. So, why argue?'

Beorn had never heard men in such a plight talking like this before. He suddenly wondered if all Northmen were not a little soft in the head.

At last the headman said, 'Look you, sailormen, what I have to do, I have to do, and there is no getting away from it. The doom was passed on you by my Council while you were still asleep. If I let you go, they would turn on me and say I was no true leader. Then I should feel the axe-kiss; and I have a wife and family to care for. I did not come all the way from Roeskilde to have my head set on a pole, I can tell you. But I will do what I can – I will have a good breakfast set before you, so that you will make the journey to Valhalla on a full stomach.'

Starkad shook his head and said, 'Do not put the cook to the trouble, friend. We have caused you enough work as it is, and to waste good food would be a crime.'

Gauk put in his word and said, 'Before we go any further, let me remind you of something. There was a rover once, called Ragnar Sheepbreeches. You have heard of him – all the world has, even the Emperor down at Miklagard. Now this Ragnar was thrown into the snake-pit when the English caught him at York, although he hinted to them that it was hardly wise to treat him that way. Do not fidget, headman, I shall tell you the tale whether you have heard it or not! Now this Ragnar told the English king plainly enough that one day his three sons would come looking for him – and they did. And when they found that king, they laid him down and cut the Blood Eagle on his back. Then they carried him round his own town of York, for all other folk to see what it was like to kill a viking. So, now you know.'

The headman shrugged his shoulders and said, 'I have known that tale since I was as old as this boy here. It is not new to me, my friend. But, mark this, there are two differences between you and Ragnar; first, we mean to put a swift end to you, with all mercy; and second, you are not kings to have young princes come revenging you. You are shipmen, no more. And I would remind you that if they had caught you at this business down in England, they would have skinned you like deer and hung your hides on the church door. So, taking it all in all, your bargain is not a bad one.'

Starkad nodded and said, 'Every man must do as he may; what more is there? But one thing I will ask of you: turn this lad loose and let him go free. It was not his fault that we brought him here to the howe.'

The headman nodded in return and said, 'I am no ogre, friend. I have a brace of boys of my own, and I know that they will always be getting into mischief, though they mean no harm in the world. That is what boys are like, and they cannot help it. So this lad shall

be untied – but I cannot turn him loose, viking. The
law of this place is that he shall be a slave, and I must
abide by the law. You know, as well as I do, that a
Danishman keeps the law, wherever he is.'

Starkad said, 'Thank you, headman. He will serve
you well.' Then he turned to Beorn and whispered,
'Don't look so hangdog, lad. Life is the thing – and
one day you'll find a way to slip out and off again. You
had wit enough to get out of Glam's clutches, didn't
you?'

Beorn felt like weeping when the villagers cut his
thongs, but he did not want to dishonour his two
friends, so he held back his tears and sat down by the
horned helmet and swords, to keep his shipmates
company as long as they needed him.

At last Starkad said, 'For the love of Odin, lad, put a smile on your face, and sing us that song about the pig to cheer the time up a little.'

Beorn sang, but his heart was not in it. The Caledonians stood glowering while he did it, wondering what strange folk these Northmen were, and shaking their dark heads, bewildered. At last Starkad said, 'That's enough, Beorn. If you can't sing more briskly than that, then be silent. You make it sound like a funeral dirge in one of these Christian churches. I don't know what has come over you.'

Then Gauk called out to the headman and said, 'I'm getting hungry, friend. Tell your axe-man to get on with it, or I shall have to put your cook to some trouble after all.'

The headman smiled and nodded to the axe-man, who took out a whetstone and started to put a good edge on the blade. While he was doing this, Gauk ignored him and said to Starkad, 'Friend, every day brings us something to learn. For years I have wondered how it feels to be dead, now I am going to find out – and that without any trouble to myself. That is the wonderful thing about it!'

Starkad said thoughtfully, 'I have wondered, as well. What puzzles me is – when the head is off, and lying on the ground, can it still think?'

Gauk scratched his own shaggy head at this, then said, 'Look, baresark, I have an idea; you see this cloak-pin in my hand? Well, after the axe-man has done his work, I will stick this pin into the oak-log if I still know anything. Will that answer your question?'

Starkad nodded and said, 'Aye, well enough, comrade. At least, if worst comes to worst, Beorn and I will know the answer, though you may not.'

Gauk smiled and said, 'Very well, so be it. I am ready with the pin. Strike now, axe-man!'

Beorn shut his eyes when the axe came down. He heard the thud and hated to look, though he was as anxious as Starkad to see what Gauk did with the cloak-pin.

But he did nothing; it lay, glimmering in the morning sun, beside the log. Starkad said, 'Well, that is another riddle answered, lad.'

Then he smiled, and turned his head towards the axe-man. 'Be about it,' he said. 'I've got a cramp starting in my right leg.'

10 Rescue

Beorn covered his face with his hands, but before he did this, Starkad nodded to him and winked as merrily as if they shared a great joke. He heard the viking say softly, 'Wait on, Gauk! I'm almost with you now, friend.'

Then all at once, the air was pierced through with loud cries and the furious buzzing of arrows. Beorn heard one thump into the log beside him, and then a deep groan. He opened his eyes again and saw the axe-man on his knees beside Gauk, fumbling at a shaft which was in his arm.

Dust rose everywhere. Feet banged on the ground. Starkad smiled and leaned over to the axe-man. 'Lend me your knife,' he said pleasantly, then cut the cords which bound his ankles.

He stood up and stretched, then flung the knife back to the wounded man, who was beyond caring whether his property was returned or not.

'Come, Beorn,' said Starkad, 'I'll take Gauk's helmet and don't you forget your sword.' Bending, he snatched up the horned helmet and longsword, and, taking Beorn by the belt, swung him on to his feet.

All happened so fast that the lad hardly knew where he was, or what had taken place.

Then, from behind the headman's thatched hut, he heard Jarl Skallagrim's voice yelling, 'Run, run! The tide is on the turn, we cannot wait for ever!'

Villagers lay tumbled beside huts and against rocks, caught by this deadly raid. Odd and Thorgaut and Skallagrim towered above a crowd of Caledonians, flailing their great axes like reeds, and hissing with every sweep, as though they were grooms polishing a horse's hide. Skallagrim saw Beorn and bawled out, 'Let's have the pig song as we go, lad. It might amuse these villagers!'

But there was no space in the air for Beorn's song, for Starkad, a pace before him, was at his own chanting, and his bull-like roar drowned all other voices.

'Up, holly-ah! Up holly-ah!'

He was setting the time for his sword-beats, and with every fall of the long blade, a man sprawled before him. A fleck of the baresark froth flew back and settled on Beorn's shoulder. He let it lie, proud to stand in Starkad's shadow now. And so they won out of Howestead and down the path to where *Reindeer* bounced on the urgent tide.

As they went, Jarl Skallagrim shouted over his shoulder, 'Never hang back like that again, Starkad. I gave you fair warning we should sail away – but my heart failed me a mile offshore and I had to come back for you, you rogue.'

He was half-glad, half-angry; glad to have Starkad back, but sad for the loss of Gauk, who had been with him all his sailing-days.

Starkad was stumbling along blank-eyed still, muttering his battle-chant, and twitching at the mouth. Beorn found it all he could do to keep up with the men, but when the rest of the villagers began to shoot arrows after them, over the cliff-top, this helped him to quicken his pace. One of the shafts struck only a yard behind him and then scuttered on, like a stone skimming over a pool, between his legs, before it came to rest against a rock.

Odd said, as he ran, 'That is a fine horned helmet, Starkad. What will you take for it? I have two bags of Frankish gold aboard ship.'

Starkad shook his head and said, 'Gauk's blood bought it, comrade. There is not enough gold in Miklagard or Jerusalem to buy this helm now. The day I give it up, I am a dead man, and the dogs can have my bones.'

So no one asked about the helmet again, and Beorn was glad that the baresark should feel so sad about their dead friend up in the village square. After that, there was little time for any sort of talking, for *Reindeer* was so anxious to be away on the ebb that she broke her moorings, and most of the vikings had to swim to gain her.

And it was just as well that they were away, for they had scarcely passed the high rock where the cormorants waited, hunched in the morning sun, when five Scottish ships-of-war came nosing round the northern headland, sails bellying, and decks crowded with bowmen.

They must have heard that *Reindeer* had put back again, and were hoping to pen her in by the shore below Howestead. But they came too late; she was not the sort of longship that waited about, once she felt the breeze in her skirts. It would have taken a Valkyr's storm-chariot to get within a javelin-cast of her now, and she skimmed the blue water as though blood pulsed in all her tarry timbers; as though she meant to go straight on, over sea, over land, over forests, until she came to stable under the golden walls of Miklagard in the distant, magic southland.

Beorn, sad as he was at Gauk's death, was jumping with excitement by the steerboard now, shouting so loudly that even Starkad put his hand over the lad's mouth and told him to stop waving his new sword about, or he would be cutting someone with it.

By middle day, they could not even see the rocky coast of Howestead, much less the ships-of-war.

'Oh, *Reindeer*, my sweeting,' sang Beorn then, laying his face on the warm planks as though the ship knew he was there, and stroking the smooth oak as a warrior strokes his horse's side.

Jarl Skallagrim already had his Latin book in his hand, but he paused a space in his reading and, turning

to Thorgaut, said with a strange smile, 'You see, shipmate, he is one of us at last. And now he will never be a
peasant again. Come, let us get on with the next
sentence; this old writing is like a blackthorn hedge
to my eyes, after our gay festival up on the rocks
there.'

11 Starkad Tamed

But it is against the will of the gods to let a man's days run too smoothly with laughter. It is the sort of pattern they will not weave, even though warp and weft seem set to pass the cloth out clean from the loom. Ten days after Howestead, *Reindeer* grew too headstrong and let herself get swept in a landward current that seemed bent on stoving her sides in on the saw-toothed rocks off Lindisfarne.

As steersman, Starkad was to blame for letting her do this thing. On some longships, among the hard-lawed Norwegians, a steersman who let his vessel hurt herself might lose his right hand, or even his head, for such a thing; but Jarl Skallagrim had never been a shipman to demand such drastic punishment.

What he did, and that only to save his face, was to put on a stern look, and say to Starkad, 'Right, Master Steersman, you know the law. Jump overboard and push her off again!'

This was said more as a joke than anything, because no man, even one as big as Thor himself, could shove a longship away from rocks. But it was the custom for this to be said among Jomsvikings, and once the steersman had gone into the water over his head, that was thought to be punishment enough for him, since no one liked getting wet.

But Starkad was so angry with himself for sailing into the sea-swirl that he lost his sense for a little while, being a baresark, and, without further word, he upped and went over the side, neck-deep in the threshing foam, with a black rock at his back and the black ship-flanks at his front. So he stood between them, pushing at *Reindeer* as though he could, in truth, have heaved her away from the shore.

But not even Starkad could do such a thing. Push as he might, she veered on her way. The men ran to the landward gunwales and stared over the banked shields down at him. The Jarl was like a madman. 'Slip sideways, man!' he yelled. 'Dive under her, or she will crush you!'

Starkad never heard him, over the crashing breakers and the screaming gulls. He stood like a hero, the bronze horns of his helmet showing now and then above the waters, and pushed with his red hands until his sinews almost parted with the strain.

Beorn was shouting at the top of his voice, pleading with Starkad to let the ship go hang, and get clear of her. Even Odd, who had few kind words to say to anyone, was on his knees like a proper Christian, clasping his crooked hands and begging Kristni Warlock to come down and pull the longship off Starkad.

But no one did that. There was a lurch of the vessel, and the softest of thuds at her side, then Beorn saw poor Starkad's feet suddenly come up over the water, and watched him being flung like a meal-sack, wet and limp, on to a small patch of pebbly shore.

Beorn gave a great cry then, and leapt after his friend. It was hard going to get through the strong waters, for they came all ways at once, but at last he was tossed on to his knees a spear's length from the baresark.

But *Reindeer* had taken it into her head to dance away now, and though the men worked at steerboard, oars and mast, they could not get her to answer to their orders. When Beorn looked up again, she was standing out two bow-shots from Lindisfarne, and still heading from the land as though Loki were pushing her at the stern. And when he looked up a third time, she was gone in a swirl of sea-fret and grey cloud and seabirds.

And there was Starkad, white and groaning, with hardly more life left in him than an empty flask; only the dregs that cling round the side. Beorn put aside all weeping now; for here was man's work. He lifted his friend's head and said, 'How is it, viking?'

Starkad was long answering, and when he did he said, 'It could be a lot better, lad.' Then he eased himself over a bit and said, 'My sword-arm is broken and I think some of my rib-planks are stove in. I'm not sure what that mad mare of a longship did to my legs, but she certainly took it out on me for treating her too nice-mouthed.'

He tried to smile, but his lips stopped half-way in their smiling and he drew in a sharp dry breath. Beorn lay across him to keep the wind away, for it was the turn of the season, and winter was coming down from Iceland with a scudding of icy grey clouds.

Along towards nightfall, Beorn said, 'Master, what can I do to help you? Shall I go up along the cliff-side and see if there are any Christmen who will come down to you here with their bandages and salves?'

Starkad said, 'Nay, never that, my son. In the days when I was a brisk Cross-breaker, I did them a lot of harm hereabouts, and it ill becomes a church-burner to go running to priests for aid, later. A man must abide by the worst of his deeds, and I will stick by mine. I know this island; when the tide ebbs, there is a causeway on to the mainland. Mayhap, if you could help me over there, we might fast a while and forage a while, and come through in the end.'

At twilight, Beorn got Starkad up with an effort and began the terrible journey to the land. The tide had nigh turned again before he dragged the Jomsviking under the lee of a rock and heaped dry weed round him for a blanket. It was a bad night, with the mews squealing and the dogs barking above them. Ten times Starkad woke and shouted that he smelled blood in the air; and every time Beorn had to wipe the cold sweat off him and coax him back to rest again.

That night snow fell for the first time in the old year, and by morning Starkad's limbs were so stiff that he begged the boy to put him below tide-level and leave him. But Beorn said firmly, 'Father, when Glam had me down on the sand and would have beaten my brains out, why did you not let him?'

Starkad said shortly, 'It ill becomes a man to let a weaker one be hurt, when by stepping in he might save him without too much trouble.'

Beorn nodded and answered, 'So is it now; but, this time, you are the weaker one, and I am one who repays a debt. We walk together from this day on, so let us have no more talk of the tides, father.'

It was only after he had said it twice, that Beorn realized what word he had used in talking to the Jomsviking.

12 Blanchland Haven

No man, drunk or sober, right-about or backwards-on, could have said but that it was a wolf's winter; and Beorn and the man were well-lucky to make haven in Alnmouth, where an old bronze-tinker took pity on crippled Starkad.

The tinker took him in and dressed his wounds, binding horse-hide round his ribs and putting his arm in a withy-splint, so that it might bend so much, but no more.

When time came for the reckoning, Starkad groaned, 'We have no coin, Master Tinker. We have only our swords and my helmet, and these we cannot part with, as you will understand.'

The tinker was a sharp fellow and said, 'That old

bronze helmet is a curiosity, sailor. It has no great value as metal, but I could put a handle on it and some good-wife would pay me my price for such a strange bucket!'

Starkad began to foam at the mouth, and Beorn knew that such talk would do him small good. So he dragged the tinker away by the arm, and in a nearby barn drew the iron stag from his tunic.

'Here, man,' he said, 'take this. A better craftsman than you will ever be cast it when the world had not yet grown its beard. A prince would be proud to have it. This is your payment.'

The tinker wiped his nose on his sleeve and said grudgingly, 'It is not a bad bit of trumpery; but I would have liked the helmet.'

Beorn said, 'If you go this way about your bargaining with my father you will get his long sword, instead; but you will not carry it away. It will carry you away. Now go.'

The man went, muttering, with Beorn's precious stag in his pouch. The boy was almost glad to find that Starkad had fainted off again, when he got back to the barn; for he hated to tell him that he had given away the Scythian treasure.

Just before Yuletide, they had gone in a wagon beyond Morpeth, and then over Tyne-river and down to Blanchland, where the snow almost filled the bowl that the village lay in. The wagon they went in belonged to a man, half-English, half-Danish, out of the old Lindsey Danelaw, in Lincolnshire, where Northmen had settled since the time of King Alfred, He was glad to have Northfolk with him for night-yarning on the southward road. Indeed, if Beorn had but said the word, Ascferth Wagoner would have taken them on down to Lincoln, where he was bound with a load of sheepskins, the wold-sheep in Lindsey having suffered a plague of foot-rot that year and all the fleeces being full of worm.

But Starkad would not budge beyond Blanchland. He said that in a dream he had seen such a place, a village in a bowl of rock, with snow all about it, and a church tower in the middle, and black pine trees round the church, and blue woodsmoke coming up from the thatched houses.

Ascferth said quietly to Beorn, 'Lad, I have three sons of my own, and I speak as a family man, you understand. So, I tell you that yon sailorman, your old father, is not long for this world. His right arm will never be straight again, and he is more like a bundle of bones than a proper-shaped man. Hark to his breathing; he can hardly put one gasp after another, he breathes as a lame man walks. So, I say, let us leave him at the church here in Blanchland, and you come on down-away with me and be my son at Lincoln. I'll pay you good hire-pence, and when the time comes, I'll set you up in a chandler's shop in Peterborough, or where you will. Is that a good bargain, then?'

Beorn looked him in the eye and said, 'Master, go your ways to Lincoln and be content. I have all the father I want; and you have all the sons you need.'

So Ascferth whipped his oxen off down the south road, and Beorn dragged Starkad into the church porch, away from the snow-blast.

They had been sheltering there a short time when the

door opened and a robed priest came out, carrying a Mass-cup. He almost fell over Starkad, who lay grunting on the tiles.

The priest said, 'By the Grail, but this man is sick, boy. Did you know that?'

He looked at Beorn with such eyes of mixed wonderment and annoyance that the lad almost laughed in his face. Yet he had sense enough to keep his bitter laughing inside himself, and said instead, 'Aye, master, he got hurt stepping off a boat. What can be done for him?'

The priest saw the sword in the sheepskin bundle, and the helmet that hung from Beorn's arm, and he said strangely, 'Why cannot you rovers rest in peace? Why cannot you see that those days are done? For God's sake, boy, that was well enough when the world was a dark place, but these days we are mostly Christmen and know what good and evil are. And yet, Mother save us, you *will* go ranting round the world with swords and helmets, as though there were still treasures to be won, and kingdoms to save.'

The priest was so angry, he almost wept. Beorn was sorry to see the state he was in, with his Christian gentleness. He had never seen a stranger take on so before about another man's affairs. He said to the priest, 'What is your name, master? I have never met such as you before, and I like to know who speaks to me.'

The priest said, 'I am Alphege, and much good may the knowing do you. Now buckle to it and give a hand with this poor daft rover, who will die before vespers if we don't get him warm.'

Behind the rude altar of the Blanchland church was a snug little crib, with hay on the floor, and a heap of skins in one corner. In the middle was a brazier, which sent out warmth from its glowing charcoal. And here they laid Starkad down and gave him warm wine that was meant for another, holier purpose. And later that night, Alphege the priest gave him boiled mutton cut into shreds, so that he could swallow it without chewing. And when Starkad lay back again, weary with feeding, in the hay, Alphege said to Beorn, 'So much can we do and no more. He sits in God's hand now. We can only pray.'

Beorn had never prayed properly before, but he knelt with Alphege before the altar-rail and put his hands together as the priest showed him. Then he listened to the words the man said, and tried to follow them; but it was hard going, and he gave up before long.

When he got up, Alphege said smiling, 'I can hear that this is as new to you as a clean shirt is to a pig, my lad. But have no fear – every man is a heathen before he learns to be a Christian.'

At another time this would have angered Beorn, but now he just nodded and tried to smile at Alphege. 'Tell me what to do, master,' he said, 'and I will do it. If Kristni will help Starkad, then Kristni is my man.'

The priest shook his head gently and said, 'What terrible fellows you Northfolk are for making bargains! You would bargain with Christ himself! But, no, he does not give his favours in return for a bargain, lad. When he helps, he helps and asks nothing. If you care to pray to him and to thank him, that is your affair, not his.'

Beorn shook his head and said, 'He is the strangest god I have heard of. Why, up north-abouts, even the dullest thrall knows that to get fish out of the sea, or apples on to the boughs, or calves from a cow, a prayer must be said to Frig, or Frey, or Odin. No prayer, no fish! It is like that.'

The priest smiled and said, 'You will learn, lad. It takes time for you Northfolk, but it comes in the end.'

They were sitting beside the sleeping Starkad, when the priest said quietly, 'There was a time, not so many lives ago, when we of Northumbria spoke just as you do now. Even the good Christmen once took Christ for a warrior-man. When I was a lad, hardly older than you are, there was an old book from which I learned my letters. It was written by a man called Cynewulf, and he made a fine set of verses about Christ. In his poem, he lets the Cross speak as the tree on which Christ was nailed. It is many years since I spoke the poem.'

Alphege walked about the little room a while, then, beating one white hand in the other to mark the time, said:

> Then the young hero, firm and unflinching,
> Stripped off his garments in sight of all men.
> Berserker rose he among all his warriors,
> Nor did his lips cry beneath hammer's rain.
> Why should I shrink then, when nails pierce my bosom?
> Why should I bow, when he held his head high?
> Proud that he held me, rude and unworthy,
> Proud would I stand again, him for to die!

Beorn was silent as Alphege finished. He thought of his own silly song about Snorre Pig, and was ashamed of it. He did not know what to say to this tall gentle priest. But suddenly Starkad spoke and said, 'I was awake, Christman, and heard your poem. If you will not bear it ill, I would say that your words were worthy of a Jomsviking, sir. And that Christ of yours sounds like a true man. That much I will give him. If a simple wooden tree will say so much for him, then I go double and will say that if he stood here now, I would take his hand.'

Alphege smiled down and nodded. 'I think he *does* stand here, Jomsviking,' he said. 'And I think he would be glad to take your hand, as well.'

They watched Starkad reach out, as though he saw the White-Christ, and they saw him clasp his hands together, as though another's hand lay in his own. Then, smiling, he rolled over into the hay and shut his eyes.

13 Blind Beacon

Spring came, and summer, and then Beorn was help-
ing the Blanchland men out on the white fells, fetching back the sheep before the winter closed in. Though
he was older now, he had known more mealtimes than
meals in the time since he left Iceland, and no one could
say that he had grown into a big boy. But he was hard
and willing, and before Christmas came, all men agreed
that he was a good-hearted lad, though a little spoiled
by the wild company he had kept.

As for Starkad, he had come through that dark winter
as well as he might, though five times he was closer to
death than the shod foot is to earth. There was an iron
in the man that kept him from faring forth, crippled
and grey though he had become. Often he would sit for

hours, stroking the horned helmet with his good left hand, and saying to himself, 'Come spring, brighthelm, and we'll be off with salt in the nostril! Aye, come the green bud and we'll be away!'

Alphege heard him one day and said to Beorn in private, 'If things do not change, the Jomsviking *will* be away, in all truth – but not to the place where he thinks he is going.'

Beorn was worried, and said, 'What can I do for him, master; what can I do? I owe him my very life.'

Alphege smiled and said, 'I think you have paid that debt, Beorn; but if you are set on doing more, then I advise that Starkad should be with someone who can tend him at all times; not with a stupid priest and a young lad, who mean well but have no skill when it comes to nursing a sick man.'

Beorn said, 'Where is there such a person, priest?'

Alphege said, 'Out on the fells, way up beyond the town and towards the sea-water, there is a widow-woman, called Katla. She is of your folk, or at least, her mother was, years ago; so she understands your ways. She is a lonely woman whose husband went into the sea five Yuletides ago when his smack turned turtle. I know she will be missing him again this Christmas. If she is willing, there is a cottage and a fire, beasts and a byre, up there on the fells, and none to share it with her. I will see her about it.'

When they first went up the high fell to her house, and Beorn saw her standing in the doorway with the rush-light behind her, for a strange moment he thought it was his mother, and his heart jumped into his throat and almost throttled him. But then he saw that she was a thin, pale-faced thing, who started away as though she was frightened of all men.

The priest consoled her and said to the others, 'You see, she has been so much alone that strangers are like wolves to her. But she will get over it, won't you, my child?'

Katla shrank by the wood wall and nodded, her tawny hair all over her face and shoulders and her dark Danish eyes staring through it, like a hare from a bush. But when she saw how truly sick Starkad was, her fear seemed to leave her, and she came forth and prepared supper for them, oat-cakes in meat broth, and barley-beer to wash it down.

The priest saw them settled in, then he blessed the house on the fell and took his leave.

Katla was a great hand with country remedies, and would spend whole days outside, gathering herbs and mashing them in a little copper cauldron she had. Starkad used to say to Beorn in secret, 'I declare, son, if I drank brewed dragon's brains it could not taste worse!'

But, all the same, the baresark never refused what she gave him and, before a month had passed, he was twice the man the ship had made him – though only half the man he used to be. Now he could walk after a fashion, without aid, and could feed himself with his left hand – his right was always bound to his body to keep it from knocking against things and hurting itself. Katla often rubbed his right arm, and would shake her reddish hair and say hoarsely, 'Do not expect too much, master. If we can get some feeling into it, that is as much as may be. You are lucky to have an arm left at all, it seems to me, for the bone was broken in many places.'

Once Starkad said, 'I used to be a fighter, woman, you may have heard. Shall I ever shake a sword with this hand again, do you consider?'

Katla said, 'If you shake a horn spoon, that will be all, master. Your sword-days are over, it seems to me.'

After she had said this, she ran away, as though afraid. And Starkad lay and stared blankly at the wood wall for two hours without speaking. Beorn came to him and said, 'Do not take on so, father. Most men would be dead and stark by now. You are fortunate.'

Starkad answered, 'Fortunate? A baresark with a horn spoon?'

Then he began to laugh and laugh till the cats ran away from the fire up a tree, and the sheep huddled together in the pen, bleating as though red-eyed Thor had come to take them for his supper. Beorn met Katla in the byre-yard and said to her hotly, 'That was no way to speak to a warrior. You have set him back with this black prattle. You have put a knitting-needle through his heart, woman.'

She went away and wept in the dairy; then Beorn was angry with himself for treating the kind woman so. He was growing tall at this time, and was beginning to feel like a man. This made him even angrier, that a grown man should talk so to a widow-woman who had given him shelter.

He was so angry with himself that he went down to Blanchland at sunset and saw the headman there, who acted for the Earl at York.

'Master,' he said, 'I am neither like lamb nor wolf,

having no trade but watching Katla's goats on the high fell. A young fellow needs work to do that will keep him on the hop. Have you a war-band in this town that I could join, and in this way earn my keep among you?'

The headman smiled gently and said, 'We keep no war-band, son, for as you see, our place lies in this little hollow and few men can find it in the winter, with snow all over it. But if they did find it, no war-band could help us, for we are in no position to defend ourselves, living like ants in a bowl, on top of one another with no room to move.'

Beorn said, 'Then what do you do when the sea-wolves come, master?'

The headman said, 'We have our ways, son. If sea-folk come, a man in a coast-village lights a beacon to warn us. Katla sees the fire and runs down here to tell me; then we all go into the church, taking what cattle we can gather into the stockade there. So we wait till the pirates go away again. A few burned houses are good value for our lives, and, besides, no sea-folk have been here for ten years. As I say, Blanchland is not easy to find, not even for raiding Scottishmen, who do not live so far away and should know where we are.'

Beorn thought a space, then said, 'Very well then, from this time, let me be your look-out man on the fells, to warn you if raiders come.'

The headman smiled and nodded. 'You have sharp eyes and are young enough to run briskly,' he said. 'Good; from now on, you are the watch-dog of Blanchland, and you shall draw the yearly fee of three sacks of oatmeal. Are you content?'

Beorn said that he was, and went back to the house

feeling that he was of some use in the world now. He came into Katla's steading quietly, so as not to disturb Starkad if he was sleeping; but a great surprise awaited him – for Starkad was well awake, and was sitting beside Katla, holding her hand and sometimes smoothing her wild hair. She was smiling faintly at him, as though she was happy to have a man near her again, after her years of loneliness.

Beorn was thunderstruck, for he had never seen Starkad as much as look at a woman before. He was also jealous, for he thought of the Jomsviking as his own man, his closest friend, his new father.

Starkad smiled at Beorn in the doorway and called out, 'Come and kiss us both, son. Katla and I have seen sense and are going to care for one another from this time on. We shall be man and wife, my son.'

These words made Beorn's mouth fall open, and he said, 'No! Oh, no!' But Starkad nodded again and said, 'Yes! Oh, yes! This good lady needs a husband, and I need a wife, to care for this broken old hulk of a body. So we shall get the priest to come up here soon and witness our handfast wedding. I cannot go into the church for it, because, to tell truth, son, I was never properly baptised, though, down at Miklagard, I often went to their Masses with the Emperor. But we Varangers in the royal guard were allowed special licence to go into church like proper Christians, so as to be near the person of the Emperor. The Greeks allowed us, in the prayers, to say "Odin" every time they said "Jesus Christ"; and to say "Freya" every time they said "Mary Mother". So I am half a Christian, though not baptised, you see!'

Beorn stood back and said angrily, 'So this is what you plot while I am away? I thought better of you, father.'

Katla smiled sadly and said, 'Come to the table, son, and drink your broth. I have thickened it with oatmeal, because I know you like that. And there is a dried onion or two for you. I kept them specially.'

Beorn glared at her and said, 'Very well, I will eat my supper, but only because I am hungry after my walk to Blanchland and back, and not because you made it for me. And, let me tell you, woman, I am no son of yours, so do not call me by that name. Starkad has the right to call me that, but not you. From this time on, I shall look after your goats and watch for the warning-beacon on the hill; so I shall earn my keep like any

other thrall. And you will call me Beorn, and nothing else. Is that understood?'

Katla stood by the table and stared at him without answering. Tears filled her eyes. Then she laid his supper and went away from the room. When she had gone, Starkad clutched the arm of his oak chair with his good left hand and screwed up his face so horribly that, if he had been strong again, Beorn would have been afraid. Then Starkad said, 'Beorn, if I were well, I would take off my belt and thrash sense into your stupid hide. Katla has done for us both what no one else would do; she has given us a home and has put food into our worthless bellies. And now you speak to her as though she is a slave, and not your mother-to-be. You treat her as though she has robbed us, not fed us.'

Beorn cried out, 'She is no mother of mine, Starkad! And she *has* robbed me, of you!'

Then he ran out without eating his broth, and spent that night among the fidgeting sheep in their cold pen.

The next morning, Starkad called Beorn to him when Katla was in the dairy, churning butter, and took him by the arm with his left hand. His face was not grim now, but deathly grave.

He said, 'Beorn, I have spent a sleepless night thinking of you. As you know well enough, I love you, and call you my son. I shall never be grateful enough for the way you saved me from the water and tended me till we came to this house. But the past is the past; and that is something that not even a king can change.'

Beorn said, 'Are you denying me, then, at last, Starkad?' He couldn't bring himself to say 'father' just then.

Starkad shook his head and said, 'God forbid that, my son. No, but I am saying to you that, now, it seems, you have grown headstrong and brisk enough to fend for yourself. I am saying that if this place is too quiet for you, then you must do what many young hounds do, and go sniffing the hedgerows for yourself. No, do not start, I am not sending you away. I am only giving you leave to live as you please; to go roving if you wish, to find yourself the sort of place that suits you, since we can both see that this steading does not. I was never one for keeping a wolf in a cage, as they do in some places. I say: Let the wolf seek his own lair and be contented there.'

Beorn was a proud boy at this time, and he did not

answer. He set his face and nodded, though deep in his heart he was sorry it had come to this after all.

Starkad said, 'A young fellow, out to make his fortune, needs a sword and a helmet. You have the sword, and now you shall have the helmet. The horned helmet that was Gauk's is yours, Beorn. If I had money to buy you a war-shirt, I would, and willingly. But you know that I own nothing but what I stand up in. Maybe you can sell your iron stag for a byrnie. You have my permission.'

Beorn almost wept to think that he had already parted with the precious stag, but he did not dare tell Starkad that, for shame.

Instead, he answered, 'Be it as you say, Starkad. I will go away, and will find what I can find. One day, I will send the price of the helmet back to you here.'

These words seemed to hurt the baresark more than anything else; but he swallowed his hurt and said, 'There is only one thing – do not leave for another week. There is something I must do, and I shall need your help in doing it. Once it is done, then the wide world is yours to go a-viking in, with my blessing.'

What Starkad wanted to do took a full week, and should, by right, have taken much more. But he had little enough time on his hands to spare, now that Beorn was set on leaving the steading on the high fell.

A thrall set a pine trunk into the ground in the stack-yard, so that it stood the height of a man, and a hand or two more. And Starkad had himself carried out there, in his chair, with his long sword in his left hand. So hour by hour he hacked at the stump, aiming his strokes this way and that, until force came back to his arm, the arm he had never used for weapon-play before. Beorn would stand, watching him, leaning at the byre-fence, seeing how, little by little, the Jomsviking was learning his trade again.

And when, at last, Starkad was satisfied that he had the mastery of the heavy blade, he called on the boy to come forward and hit at him with a stout blackthorn, as though they were in conflict together. Now Beorn hated to do this, fearing to hurt Starkad; but the man grew so angry at his refusal that in the end Beorn gave in.

At first, many of his blows landed on Starkad's shoulders; but, at last, Beorn found that try as he might he could not touch the baresark. And when this lesson was learned, Starkad ordered him to strike anywhere, up or down, so as to bring nimbleness back to his legs.

Many a crack Beorn gave him on the shins using the viking leg-blow; then came the day when Starkad laughed in the newly-bright air, for the year had turned now. And on that day he waited until Beorn swiped out at his legs, judged the blow like a hawk watching a partridge, then brought down the long sword so fast that it was only a gleam of silver in the sunlight. The thick blackthorn staff fell in two halves at Beorn's feet.

Starkad put up his sword and came to him, smiling quietly. He placed his good arm round the boy's shoulders and said, 'Very well, lad, so this is the day you can count yourself a free rover. Now that I can manage my old trade this new way, there is nothing more to keep you here. Eat and sleep well this night,

and tomorrow I will set you on your way, and may life
use you well!'

When Starkad had gone into the house to slake his
thirst with the last of the October ale, Beorn suddenly
found himself weeping, and went quickly from the
steading so that none of the thralls should see his
weakness. It is one thing, he thought, to *dream* of
freedom; but it is another to take it when it is offered.

Now, all at once, he saw Starkad and even Katla in a
new way, as all the world he had, as his own folk. And
he saw this steading on the high fell as his only home.
All else in the world was unknown and unsure. Perhaps
he would be going to his death, or at least to misery;
whereas, up here on the hill, there were love and kind-
ness and a hearth-fire to sit by. But he had spoken his
word, and since he had journeyed with Jomsvikings, he
had learned that, once a man does this, there is no going
back.

Up on a little hummock that the Blanchland-folk still
called Grimshowe, under a wind-writhen hawthorn
tree, Beorn sat down and let the twilight wrap itself
round him like a thin cloak. And there, with the
curlews crying and the sheeps' sad bleating in his ears,
he thought of all that had passed, and tried to guess at
all to come. Some things that he thought brought tears
to his eyes, and as dusk fell, he put his hands to his eyes
to wipe the salt water away.

It was while his face was covered so, that the distant
beacon up above the coast flared a dull red for a
while, and then died down again. It was the warning he
had sworn to watch for, but which, in his own time of
trouble, he never saw. If he had seen it, he would have

raced like a wild deer down into Blanchland, to shout out from the church steps that the sea-rovers were on their way again. But such words were never said, and Beorn went back to the steading without knowing he had failed the folk who trusted him.

14 New Guardian

It was a good send-off meal of barley cakes, cow-meat, dried beans, and honey-ale. Katla lighted five white wax candles in his honour, though she had meant to give them to the church at Easter. Good pine logs crackled in the hearth, and that evening the steading was as warm as any home could be.

There was a shaggy grey and white sheepdog called Nim, and though he had come to adore Starkad above all men, even Nim seemed sad that Beorn was leaving. It was as though he had got the news by some secret way, as bees do when their keeper dies. He curled up in a far, dim corner and whimpered to himself – a thing he never reckoned to do usually. But tonight was different for them all.

Katla leaned across the board-table gently and said, 'You may not wish to call me mother, but you cannot stop me from thinking of you as my son, Beorn. And I know that there is sadness in your heart, even though you try to hide it.'

Beorn put on a smile.

'If it pleases you, Katla,' he answered, 'I *will* call you mother, for this last night.'

Truth to tell, he was glad she had spoken thus, and glad to call her mother. She smiled and helped him to more meat and ale. Then she said, 'Your heart is heavy at the journey that lies before you. But you will find new courage as you fare forth into the world and conquer it, inch by inch. Not so many years ago, down among the Essex-folk, there was a good old fighter named Byrhtwold. And when the Danishmen came ashore at a place called Maldon, and killed Byrhtwold's lord after a hard fight, this old warman spoke up and said these words:

> "*Thought shall be the harder, heart the keener,*
> *Courage the greater, as our strength faileth.*
> *Here lies our leader, in the dust of his greatness.*
> *Who leave him now, damned be for ever.*
> *I, who am old now, will not leave this battle,*
> *But will lie at his feet, in the dust with my leader.*"'

Then she stopped, as though she was a little ashamed, a mere woman speaking so. But her words had moved Beorn, and he took her hand and said, 'I understand, mother. You are telling me that a man must have courage at all times, whatever the odds. Is that it?'

Katla rose from the board and put her hands to her face.

'I do not know *what* I am trying to tell you, son,' she said. 'I think it was the honey-ale talking, not me.'

As the two men looked up at her from the table, the night outside was suddenly cracked across with harsh high cries. Then a horn blew as though the day of judgement had come and a voice called loudly, 'Open the gates, you within! Open them, or we shall break them down!'

Starkad looked across at Beorn's white face and said, 'There is no need to ask what manner of men stand outside our stockade, son. You and I both know what such a greeting means.'

He hobbled to where his sword stood by the wall, then turned and said, 'Will you give me leave to wear your horned helmet for the last time?'

Beorn nodded, his tongue silent. And the Joms-viking said, 'It is strange that they did not light the beacon on the coast-hill to warn us we might expect such visitors.'

Beorn stared at him, silently, and then took up his own short sword and went over to where Starkad stood, wrapping a sheepskin round his right arm in place of a shield.

As the shouting grew louder outside, the baresark said to Katla, 'At least we have fed well, wife, and good food is always worth two men. We count for four, you see! Now, Beorn, if you are coming out with me, to try a few of the tricks we have practised these last days, then I must ask you to stand, as old Gauk the Guardian did, at my back. So, you will protect me there, and you will also be out of the way if I flail about me a little wildly – as I am well apt to do when the game gets hot. Will you be my Guardian, then?'

Beorn fell on to his knees before Starkad and took his left hand and pressed it to his lips. 'Father,' he said, 'this is greater honour than when a chief gives a ring to his warrior, for me to take Gauk's place. If I never gain more fame than this, I shall go to the last resting-home happy.'

But Katla had run into the corner, where Nim the dog stood bristling, and put her rough apron over her head, weeping that she had found a family at last only to lose it again.

Starkad gave a dry cough or two, but did not go to her. Instead, he turned to Beorn and said, 'Come on, then, son, and let us see what sort of weather it is outside. It should be warming up a little, at this time of the year.'

And so they went through the cottage door, and shut it fast after them.

gaily, like grooms to the wedding, and not fearfully, like beasts to the knacker's shed.'

He slapped Beorn lightly on the back with his sword-flat, and said, 'Come to think of it, lad, this is what it has all been leading up to. This is why I saved you from Glam that day, on the Iceland shore, so that you would be by me when the ravens came at last for their pickings. Oh, I could wish no better! I have had a goodish life, and now that I am no use for anything but the hearth, it is just as well that I should be called out into the moonlight with my son behind me and a good sword in my hand. Fight well, Beorn, and no man can ask for anything more of you. If one of them gets behind me, through the gateway, don't call me, to make me turn round and take my eye off the others; just deal with him as best you can. Strike sideways, not down, for you stand better chance of getting him that way. And, just one more thing, strike hard, though it may go against the grain. For a half-lamed Northman is worse than anything; he knows it is to be his end soon, and before he goes, he will take even a wolf with him, though he has nothing but his teeth to use. Good luck to your sword, and, when you hear the "Up-holly-ah!" never give a thought to me, for I shall be well away at my old trade.'

The tears were running down Beorn's cheeks, but he was not sad; his heart was overflowing with all manner of feelings, and tears were the only words that would come to him. He gave Starkad a slap on the back as they went to open the gates; and that was all he said to his foster-father. But it was enough.

As they drew the wood-bolts, a great voice from the

other side bawled out, 'And time, too! We thought you were saying a saga to one another in there! Come on out now, and either tell us the way down to Blanchland, or give us the satisfaction of sword-play.'

Starkad called back, 'You'll get no good word from us, sea-wolf; only the edge of two swords. Take which one you wish, they are both keen.'

Torches were flaring outside and men were jostling and laughing. As Starkad flung the gate wide and leaned his wounded right side against the post, Beorn saw the dull gleam of iron-mesh in the moonlight, and his eye counted more than a dozen men, with swords and axes ready. A big man in a dark bearskin, their leader, was first to step forward. He waved to his fellows to stand back and give him first knock.

'Come on, grandad,' he called to Starkad, 'I do not think we shall be long about our visit, somehow! A grey-beard and a lad are small fences for Jomsvikings to leap.'

Beorn felt his skin prickle at these words; but they seemed to have no effect on Starkad, who set his mouth firmly, and, as the big man swung sideways, thrust out at point's length with the long sword.

'Up holly-ah!' shouted Starkad, with a bark like a dog.

The man in the bearskin gave a sharp cry, and staggered back, his hand to his cheek. 'By Odin,' he said, 'but I know only one man who could sneak through my guard that way, and he died against Holy Island, almost two years ago, trying to hoist a longship back into the currents!'

Then, as he began his next rush, Starkad suddenly

flung down his long sword and yelled out, 'Skallagrim! By all the gods, Jarl Skallagrim!'

Beorn's eyes nearly jumped from their lids, to see the big man fling down his own weapon and throw back his helmet. Then the two men had arms about each other, and were stumbling round in the moonlight as though they were drunk. Odd and Thorgaut, and half a dozen others from *Reindeer*, were beside Beorn now, slapping his back so hard that they almost stunned the boy.

And at last Skallagrim shouted, 'We've found the luck of *Reindeer* again, by the grace of Odin! The lad who can sing us Snorre Pig! Oh, lad, what a treasure – when all we hoped to gain were a few old cups and fiddle-faddles from Blanchland kirk!'

After he had laughed a while longer, and the first greeting was over, he called out, 'Come away with us, lads, and off to sea again! We'll find other pickings nearer York; and they say the Humberside men are mighty careless with their cattle these days. That's where we'll go!'

But Starkad shook his head and said, 'My sailing-days are past, Jarl. Come inside and let my wife set food and drink before you. Let us talk of old times. Then be on your way before I change my mind and shorten you all by a head's length!'

So they met again, and Jarl Skallagrim's folk feasted so well that they cleaned out Katla's stock for many a day. And when they had finished, the Jarl rose and said, 'Lady, I think this Starkad-Baresark is not as daft as he seems. If I had a little farm-steading like this, I might well give up the salt-life myself. But what will be, will be. I must go my way, and it would ill become us to

be found snoring here by dawntime. The Blanchland men might not welcome us quite as well as you have done. So, off we go, and good luck to you all. No longship-crew shall ever bother you again while my name stands for anything on the northern seas.'

Then it was that Beorn stepped forward and said, 'Master Jarl, I was almost on my way to seek my fortune when you came. It now seems to me better bargaining with fate to go with folk I know, than to tread a lone wolf's track through the woods.'

Jarl Skallagrim said nothing, but gazed first at Starkad and then at Katla. And when he had seen what was in their sad faces, he turned to Beorn and said, 'On your own head be it, viking. There is a sea-chest for you to sit on, in *Reindeer*, if your heart is in this thing. I say no more.'

Before dawn, they had gone and the good folk of Blanchland never even knew that they had had visitors in the night.

16 Golden Hair

Years go by, and there is no stopping them. They are the wheels on a wagon, always turning while there is an ox to draw them. Trees grow towards the sky, then fall, their roots rotten. They mix with the earth and new trees rise from them. That is how it goes.

Now Nim was so old that he scarcely ever left the steading, and the youngest lamb could outrun him. Now his eyes were dim, and he had to live by his nose and his ears. But they were still sound enough. So keen, they were, that Nim often knew when a man was coming, long before old Starkad could see him on the hill path, long before Katla could hear him, even, and her ears were as sharp as they had ever been, though she was bent and wrinkled now.

So it was that, one bright summer morning, when the

larks were rising above the steading as though they adored the place, Nim began to whimper, then to growl, then to bark. He rose from his corner and tottered on stiff legs to the doorway, sniffing mightily.

Katla with a ladle in her hand, said, 'What ails the dog?'

Starkad, greasing a pair of new leather leggings by the hearth, said, 'It must be the season that has got into his blood. I've not heard him make a whimper for weeks!'

And suddenly, as they watched, old Nim ran across the stack-yard like a young puppy, and then began to bark and bark as though he had been visited by Freya and given the secret of endless youth. Starkad was about to go out and quieten the dog, because he had got so that sudden noises upset him; but as he rose from his chair, the yard-gate flew open as though a giant had pushed it, and there stood a man whose hair flamed out in the sunshine like red gold.

He had no sword in his hand, no helmet on his head, but only a great blackthorn staff that thumped on the ground with every step he took, as though he was Thor come again and wanted to tread everything flat, to show his strength.

To tell the truth, Starkad was a little afraid at this man. The baresark years had faded like a dream, had gone like last October's ale, and were but a dim memory. Now Starkad saw only a strong young giant carrying a staff that would have laid Skallagrim himself flat on the ground, even in his prime. So Starkad and Katla put their arms round one another and waited for the worst this tall stranger might bring.

They did not dare even look into his bearded face as he came towards them. Then they saw his black shadow kneeling, and felt his oak-firm arms about them. And they looked down a little way into a face they knew, but strong now, hard like a god's face, and like a great man's face.

And Beorn smiled up at them, out of his thick golden beard, and said, 'I have come back, mother. I have come to serve you, father. Is that good?'

Starkad's skin crawled with the old baresark feeling, and he said quietly, 'Yes, it is not bad. I have known worse.'

But in the deep of his stone heart, he could have cried and cried with joy. He felt a child now, he felt like blind old Nim in the stack-yard; Nim who was telling the lambs that now Beorn was back they had best mind their manners and treat a dog with respect.

Then Beorn lifted them both off their feet and set them down in their chairs by the hearth-fire. With a strange look, he said to them, 'I have a bag of Miklagard gold for you in the cart that follows; and a king's crown for my father. But there is a confession to make.'

Starkad put on his worst face, the tears running into his grey old beard though. 'Well,' he barked, 'out with it, my lad!'

Beorn said, 'I threw the short sword and the horned helmet into the sea off Jomsburg as we came by. I thought that made a good end to it all. The viking days are done.'

Starkad thought a while, then said, 'Aye, boy, that's good enough. They served their turn. And even they must finish when their time comes.'

Beorn said, his face turned away, '*Reindeer* is out on the Portage, and the Patzinaks have her for their palace. All the others are in a howe at Hedeby. I came back in a Frankish trader, *The Maid of Aachen*. Not the way I like to travel, but beggars cannot be choosers, father.'

Starkad thought a while, then smiled and said, 'Nay, that they cannot. You've done fairly well for a silly young lad. Mayhap, when the new year comes, I'll try to knock a bit of husbandry into your thick head. This farming is real man's work, not like that fly-by-night roving, and that baresark foolery men set such store by. Are you willing to learn, lad?'

Beorn's arms were round Katla, and he was trying to mop up her tears on his silken sleeve. He spared a glance for Starkad, and said, 'Aye, I'm willing, father. But go easy with me, my hands are soft. I'm only a viking, you must remember, not one of you hard-fisted farmers.'

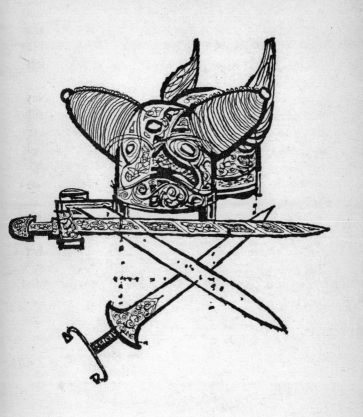

also by Henry Treece

THE CHILDREN'S CRUSADE

A brilliantly imagined story based on the tragic crusade of 1212, when 30,000 children followed a twelve-year-old shepherd boy on his pilgrimage to the Holy City.

LEGIONS OF THE EAGLE

A stirring story of a boy living and fighting at the time of the first major Roman invasion of Britain.

VINLAND THE GOOD

A moving tale, based on incidents from two Icelandic sagas, *Eirik the Red* and *The Greenland Saga*.

SWORDS FROM THE NORTH

Stirring adventures of Viking mercenaries under Harald Hadrada in the Byzantine Empire.

A Viking Saga
VIKING'S DAWN, THE ROAD TO MIKLAGARD, VIKING'S SUNSET

The three books tell the tale of Harald Sigurdson, who sailed with the Vikings in search of treasure and endured icy seas, incredible hardships and bloodthirsty resistance.

THE EAGLE OF THE NINTH *Rosemary Sutcliff*

Twelve years earlier, Marcus' father, with the Ninth Hispana Legion – 6,000 men – had marched beyond Hadrian's Wall, and nothing had ever been seen or heard of them again. Marcus had always been sure that only some dreadful disaster had prevented his father's return, not the cowardice that some people hinted at.

And now at last, invalided out of the Roman Army after his first and only battle as a Centurion, he is given permission by the Legate of the Sixth Legion to follow his father north and perhaps find out at last how the Ninth Legion had met its end. Above all, Marcus hoped he might discover what had happened to the Eagle, the standard of the Legion and symbol of its honour.

THE COURAGE OF ANDY ROBSON *Frederick Grice*

All his life Andy had lived with the lights and the sounds of the Sleet-burn colliery and now, transplanted far north to stay with his aunt and uncle, Andy felt lost and lonely in the quietness of the country. His uncle was Park Warden to Lord Hetherington's estate, and so responsible for the well-being of the famous wild white cattle of Lilburn. His work wasn't made any easier by the rude and uncaring attitude of Lord Hetherington himself, who regarded the cattle as mere irritations. Then disaster struck, not just once, but twice, and Andy found himself forced to draw on reserves of strength and courage that he hadn't realized he possessed.

JOHN DIAMOND *Leon Garfield*

William Jones's father is dying, and only the boy knows the great
secret of his father's life: that he was a swindler who had made his
fortune by cheating his old business partner, Diamond. Haunted by this
terrible knowledge, young William sets out from the country for London
all alone – to find Diamond and lay his father's ghost. But London
is less than welcoming, and his alarming experiences in the streets
of Holborn and Limehouse soon teach him that even the distinction
between enemy and friend can be unclear ...

ISLAND OF THE BLUE DOLPHINS *Scott O'Dell*

Based on the true story of an Indian girl who was abandoned on a
fierce and desolate island off the coast of California and survived alone
for eighteen years. She was known as the Lost Woman of San Nicolas.

Karana was only twelve years old when her tribe was betrayed by the
Aleutian sea-otter hunters; when the handful who were not murdered
were taken from the harsh rock which was their home, and she stayed
behind to search for her young brother. After his tragic death she
lived a Robinson Crusoe life, entirely alone, battling with wild
animals, hiding from the marauding Aleutians, scrounging for food
and taming a wild dog to be her only company.

A Newbery Award winner, for 12 years and upwards.

Heard about the Puffin Club?

... it's a way of finding out about Puffin books and authors, of winning prizes (in competitions), sharing jokes, a secret code, and perhaps seeing your name in print! When you join you get a copy of our magazine, *Puffin Post*, sent to you four times a year, a badge and a membership book.

For details of subscription and an application form, send a stamped addressed envelope to:

The Puffin Club Dept A
Penguin Books Limited
Bath Road
Harmondsworth
Middlesex UB7 ODA

and if you live in Australia, please write to:

The Australian Puffin Club
Penguin Books Australia Limited
P.O. Box 257
Ringwood
Victoria 3134